ARCHON

AR

CHON

Lana Krumwiede

CANDLEWICK PRESS

Copyright © 2013 by Lana Krumwiede

First paperback edition 2015

Library of Congress Catalog Card Number 2013943066
ISBN 978-0-7636-6402-2 (hardcover)
ISBN 978-0-7636-7659-9 (paperback)

14 15 16 17 18 19 BVG 10 9 8 7 6 5 4 3 2 1

Printed in Berryville, VA, U.S.A.

This book was typeset in Berkeley Oldstyle Medium.

Candlewick Press
99 Dover Street
Somerville, Massachusetts 02144

visit us at www.candlewick.com

To the amazing Molly Jaffa,
without whom this book would not exist

• • •

ONE

Even the fiercest warrior will be tortured with moments of regret and sorrow. Let them wash over you like cleansing waters. Do not absorb them.

— THE WARRIOR'S SERENITY

A throng gathered around the hauler as it inched through the city of Deliverance. Taemon was in the passenger seat, Amma was in the middle, and Drigg was driving. Or trying to, anyway. The press of desperate people made it difficult.

"We need food!" someone called.

"It's all going to the Relief Center!" Taemon yelled. "You can get food there."

The mob's fervor increased.

"There's never enough!"

"My children . . ."

"Is there any milk in there?"

Taemon leaned out the window and searched the crowd for his parents, as he had done for the past four months while accompanying Drigg on his weekly trips bringing food to the city dwellers who had decided to stay put after the Fall—the day psi mysteriously disappeared from Deliverance.

It was hard to believe that Deliverance had been clean, orderly, and impressive just four short months ago. Now it was a filthy, bedraggled heap—a shadow of its former glory.

Some of the damage was due to the earthquake that had rocked the city on the day of the Fall. But most of the destruction was a result of the riots that had occurred in the weeks afterward. Once people had lost their telekinetic abilities, their lives were completely upended. Their vehicles didn't work. They had to kick down their own front doors to enter their homes. Even the simplest of tasks—cooking, dressing, and hygiene—had to be reinvented using nothing but their hands. For people who had been taught that manual labor was beneath them, the situation was appalling.

While the violence had died down, the quality of life had yet to improve much for the thousands of people still living in the city. Food was frightfully scarce—the spring crops had withered because people could not figure out how to water that many plants without psi. Volunteers from the colony tried to help, but the city dwellers still hadn't grasped the fact that psi was gone for good. It made Taemon sick to see so many city dwellers stand by uselessly while their food supply was ruined rather than adopting the tools and techniques of the colonists. It seemed people would rather go hungry than accept the truth.

But for Taemon, hardest of all was the knowledge that the destruction, the anger, and the hunger were all his fault. Because he had caused the Fall.

Four months ago, the Heart of the Earth had given him a choice: accept his role as the True Son and do what was best for the people, or turn his back on his destiny and become an instrument of war. It wasn't much of a choice. Taemon had directed the Heart of the Earth to do away with psi, the telekinetic power that had become a weapon in the hands of the corrupt. He'd believed he was ushering in a new era—an era of peace and equality. He had pictured the people of Deliverance living in harmony with the people of the colony, learning from their powerless brethren how to live a new kind of life, one that would bring them closer to the Heart of the Earth—and closer to the teachings of the Prophet Nathan.

Instead, the people of Deliverance had clung to their old beliefs and were praying for the day when this punishment would be lifted and they could go back to a life free of labor.

Only Taemon and Amma knew that no such day was coming.

Still, every week, he made himself go with Drigg to the city, where he had to confront the repercussions of his decision, in the hope that he would find Mam and Da. Or find someone who knew where they were, and maybe get word of them. So far, though, nothing.

Taemon rolled up the window and sat back in his seat. "Will it ever get better?"

Amma sighed. "Someday. It has to get better someday."

"I'm just happy if I don't run anybody over with the hauler," Drigg said.

Taemon watched a man who walked beside the truck as it crept along. He looked like most city dwellers since the

Fall: hair matted, shirt rumpled and dirty, psi collar ripped out and replaced by yarn ties crudely laced through the fabric, psi cuffs torn off, psi shoes bound with strips of cloth to keep them on his feet. This was the new uniform of the people of Deliverance.

"After we unload all this, I've got a list of things to pick up in the city." Drigg's voice cut through Taemon's gloomy mood. "It'll take me a couple of hours, and if you want to take some time to look for your folks, that'd be all right."

"Thanks, Drigg," Taemon said. "There's still one asylum I haven't checked."

They found the asylum, a grim, squat building secluded in a woodsy area and surrounded by an iron fence.

Drigg drove into a gravel parking lot that held a few abandoned quadriders. He stopped the hauler at the gate, which led to a long path lined with spindly pine trees. "Now, listen: when I get back to pick you up, you have to be watching for me. I can't leave the hauler to go looking for you."

Taemon nodded. The hauler had come from the powerless colony, which had only a handful of corn-fueled vehicles. Now they were the only vehicles in all of Deliverance that still worked. If they left the hauler unattended, someone would surely steal it. "Right," said Taemon. "Thanks."

"I'm coming with you," Amma said, scooting across the front seat. "Unless you need my help with your errands, Drigg?"

"Nah, you go on with the boy. Keep an eye on him."

Taemon was grateful for the company. The abandoned asylums were even more disturbing than the rest of the city. Even though he'd never seen an asylum before the Fall, he couldn't help but think they had always been disturbing.

He forced his feet to move forward, stepping on the thin shadows that the trees cast across the path. He told himself that each shadow he passed brought him closer to his family — or what was left of it.

His brother was gone, buried under the stones when the temple collapsed during the Fall. There was no way to bring Yens back, but he could find his parents. He had to.

"This is the last place I know to look," Taemon said.

"We'll find them," Amma said. "Other families got separated during the Fall. It takes time, but they find each other."

Taemon nodded, trying to keep his spirits up despite the unsettling sights ahead: the overgrown shrubs and grass, the cracked sidewalk, the walls streaked with water stains, the roof sagging in several places. The disrepair had clearly started long before the Fall. "Skies, I hate these places."

Amma shuddered. "I know."

Before the Fall, anyone who was deemed too dangerous was sent to an asylum. Usually *dangerous* meant that their powers were abnormal, which Taemon now knew meant they simply had one of the rarer types of psi, like precognition or telepathy, but it could also mean their behavior was odd or violent. In the asylum, these people were medicated heavily to suppress their psionic abilities. Toward the end of his reign, Elder Naseph had used asylums as a handy way of silencing anyone who opposed him. That included Da, Taemon had learned, who'd become more and more vocal in his opposition to Naseph's warmongering ways. Mam had been deemed guilty by association.

The front door was wide open and askew, the top hinge long since missing. Taemon knocked on the door frame, a gesture that still felt a bit foreign to him, though he'd been functioning without psi for months before the Fall. "Hello?

Anyone here?" He leaned inside the door and called again. "Hello?" His voice echoed inside the entryway.

He glanced at Amma. "Looks pretty empty, just like the others."

"There could be some squatters inside. They might know something."

"Squatters usually don't want to be found," Taemon said.

They stepped inside, the grit-covered linoleum scratchy underfoot. A wide staircase led down to what may have been a common room for the patients to gather in. Chairs, sofas, and lamps, many of them broken, were piled in random places. They'd seen the same disarray in the other asylums.

"Why is the furniture always thrown around like that?" Amma said.

"Looting, maybe?" Taemon guessed. "During the Fall?"

"What would they be trying to loot? The drugs in here are used to take psi away, not bring it back."

Taemon grunted. He tried to picture the chaos that must have erupted when the people who ran this place realized they no longer had psi. There would have been no way to keep the doors locked, no way to subdue the inmates. He looked again at heaps of broken furniture. Barricades. Fighting. The image of it came perfectly to his mind, squashing his hopes for finding Mam. "Is anyone here? We're looking for a former inmate. We won't cause any trouble."

A scuffling sound startled them, but it was only a bird trapped inside, fluttering against the ceiling.

They went from door to door and found no one. There was no electricity, but there were windows, small and high, next to the ceiling. They let in enough natural light to see the same things they'd seen in other asylums: bizarre scratch marks on many of the walls, odd designs or symbols that held no meaning for Taemon. Beds and chairs were turned on end in strange places.

"So sad," Amma said. And she was right. Everything about this place was sad.

They checked every room, but there were no signs of habitation.

"We can search the grounds," Amma said as they neared the end of the last hallway. "There might be people hiding in the woods."

Taemon looked down the hall one last time and saw a door they hadn't noticed before. "Hold on. There's one more room."

He jogged to the door and tried to push it open, but something was blocking the way. Leaning his shoulder into the door, he pushed harder.

The door gave way with a smash, but it still didn't open all the way. Taemon peered into a dim storage room. Shelves filled with cleaning supplies, linens, and medicine lined the walls. One shelf held a stash of food and drink pouches. Brooms and mops were propped up against the far wall.

Amma had her hand on his shoulder, trying to get a look. "We need more light," she whispered.

Taemon tried to open the door wider, but something was blocking it. It looked like a chair had been braced against the door and been broken when he'd forced it open. One large piece remained wedged between the door and the wall. He stepped into the tiny room to clear the debris.

"Two yellow, one blue, three red," a hoarse voice whispered from a dark corner. "Two yellow, one blue, three red."

"Hello?" Cautiously, Taemon moved toward the sound of the voice. "We're here to help."

"Two yellow! One blue! Three red!" The tone was more frantic now.

"I didn't mean to upset you," Taemon said. "I'll pick up this mess."

A thin figure in a dingy, shapeless dress darted forward and got to the chair before Taemon did. She leaned over the furniture pieces, her lank hair covering her face. "Don't worry," she said. "I'm here. You are broken, but you'll get better."

Gently she gathered the splintered wood in her arms, cradling it as she moved toward the opposite wall. She arranged the pieces thoughtfully among the mops and brooms. "Two yellow. One blue. Three red," she muttered. Then she turned to face Taemon.

It was Mam.

Thin, sunken cheeks. Matted hair. Eyes that appeared cloudy and vacant.

But it was Mam.

"Mam!" he tried to say, but the lump in his throat turned it into little more than a gasp.

She smiled at him, looking more like herself.

"Mam, I can't believe it's you! I've been looking everywh—"

"Two yellow. One blue. Three red."

"What? Mam, it's me. Taemon."

She smiled again, but Taemon realized that the smile wasn't for him. It was a vacant smile, void of recognition. She turned and busied herself with something on the shelf.

Amma stepped up beside him. "It's okay," she whispered. "We'll take her back to the colony, and the healers will help her."

Taemon nodded, fighting to breathe past the despair that pressed on his chest.

"She's alive," Amma said. "That's what's important."

Mam turned around with something in her hand. She held it out for Taemon and Amma to see. Pills. Different sizes, different colors. He stared at the pills in Mam's hand for a frozen moment before he understood: two yellow, one blue, three red.

"No!" He lunged toward her.

She was too quick. She brought her hand to her mouth, and the pills were gone.

"Mother of Earth," Taemon whispered. "She's been taking those horrible drugs this whole time."

Amma stepped past him and gathered all the medicine bottles. "We need to get rid of these."

With no trash can in sight, they ended up piling the bottles in the corner behind the door to keep them out of Mam's reach.

Meanwhile, Mam seemed more interested in the mops and brooms that were lined against the wall. She stroked the strands of the mop and plucked dust bits off the broom bristles, murmuring to herself all the while.

Taemon spoke as gently as he knew how. "Mam, we came to help you. Where's Da? Do you know?"

"You'll be fine," Mam murmured, but she wasn't looking at Taemon. She was still inspecting the broom. "Just fine. I'll take care of you."

Taemon and Amma exchanged a worried look.

"Wouldn't you like to come with us?" Amma said. "We'll take you to a safe place."

Mam didn't respond.

"Mam?" Taemon put his hand on her back. "What happened? Where's Da?"

She shrugged his hand away and glared at him, then turned back to the broom. "Don't worry. I won't leave you here alone. I'll take care of you."

Taemon stepped back. "What do I do?" he whispered to Amma.

Amma looked as helpless as he felt. "I don't know. If we can get her back to the colony, she might—"

"They took him away," Mam said suddenly. "They took him."

The words filled the tiny room even though Mam's voice was barely audible.

"You mean Da?" Taemon asked. Somehow he managed to keep his voice soft and relaxed.

"They took Darling away," Mam said. Then she looked up, and for a moment Taemon thought she recognized him.

"Where, Mam? Where did they take him?"

"They took him to the Republik," she said, her eyes back on the floor. "They made him go. They said if he didn't . . ." She hugged herself and began to moan. When she looked up again, her eyes were vacant.

"Two yellow. One blue. Three red." She looked toward the shelves.

"No more drugs," Amma said gently. She turned to Taemon. "We have to get her out of here."

"I can't leave," Mam said. "I can't! They need me." She clutched a broom and mop close.

"I need you, too," Taemon said. "Please, Mam."

A horn sounded from outside. One long honk, then two short ones.

"That's Drigg," Taemon said. "We have to go."

Mam moaned again, louder this time.

"I know!" Amma said, stepping forward. "We can take them with us." She started gathering mops and brooms.

"Brilliant!" Taemon said, moving to do the same.

"Stop!" Mam shrieked. "Leave them alone! They've done nothing!"

Amma and Taemon froze as Mam carefully replaced each mop and broom.

"What are we going to do?" Amma asked just as Drigg's horn sounded again.

Taemon and Amma exchanged a look. They seemed to come to the same conclusion at the same time. Quickly, before she could react, they each took hold of one of Mam's arms and half dragged her into the hallway. She was so thin, so frail. She hollered and squirmed, but she was too weak to struggle very much.

They moved as quickly as was possible with Mam resisting. It was a long way back to the parking lot: down hallways, around corners, across the big room, up the stairs, and, finally, through the front door.

Halfway across the cracked sidewalk, he looked up and saw the hauler waiting for them. Mam must have seen it, too, because she chose that moment to dig in her heels with a vengeance.

That's when they tripped.

Taemon went down hard, skinning his palms, but Mam took the worst of it. She landed on her back, and her head hit the sidewalk with a sickening crack.

Taemon knelt next to Mam. She looked at him, her breathing shallow, the black centers of her eyes wide and deep.

"Mam? Are you okay?"

"Darling Houser," she said. "Find him."

"Mrs. Houser?" Amma shook Mam's shoulder. "Stay awake, okay? We're taking you to see your sister."

Will Mam even remember that she has a sister? Taemon wondered vaguely. They'd been separated as children, his aunt Challis sent to live in the powerless colony when it was discovered that she possessed unusual—and therefore dangerous—powers. He wondered what sort of behind-the-scenes negotiations had resulted in Challis's being sent to the colony rather than to an asylum.

Regardless, Taemon had grown up believing that his aunt had died at the age of four. Would Mam remember the truth?

Taemon looked up when he heard footsteps crunching down the path. Drigg was running toward them.

"I'll carry her," he said. "You go back to the hauler."

Drigg picked up Mam, and the four of them continued down the path. Taemon hurried ahead to the gate. As he held it open for the others, he heard a sound that made his stomach twist.

The hauler.

Taemon watched their only source of transportation speed away without them, spitting gravel as it went.

TWO

There will come a moment when despite all your training, all your studies, all your knowledge, you will be unable to find a solution. And yet you will know the solution. Forget everything, and you will remember it.

— THE WARRIOR'S SERENITY

Drigg eased Mam off his shoulder and laid her gently on the grass before he started cursing. "Blazing skies in the morning! I thought it would be safe for a few seconds. I didn't see anyone nearby."

"I think there are people hiding in the woods," Amma said. "I got that feeling when we first came here."

Taemon knelt to check on Mam. She was out cold. Amma crouched next to him. "Is she sleeping?" Taemon asked. All the excitement and struggling had probably worn her out.

"I think she's unconscious," Amma said. "We need to get her to the healers as quickly as possible."

Drigg rubbed the bald spot on his head. "It's at least a day's walk to the colony. And sundown's in a couple hours."

"Then we'd better start walking," said Taemon.

Drigg looked longingly at the quadriders that had been abandoned in the parking lot after the Fall. Taemon knew exactly what Drigg was thinking because he thought the same thing every time he saw the useless quadriders. They were surrounded by vehicles that no one could drive again.

"I hate to say this," Drigg said, "but maybe we should stay here for the night and get an early start in the morning."

"I'm not spending the night in that place." Taemon shuddered.

"I'm with Taemon on this one," Amma said. "Besides, if people really are living in the woods around here, we may not be safe overnight."

Taemon turned back toward the asylum. "I'll go find something to carry Mam with."

"I'll see if I can find any food pouches," Amma added as she followed.

•   •   •

It had been fully dark for at least an hour before they agreed to stop. Drigg had put together a stretcher from some poles and rough canvas Taemon had found at the asylum. They had taken turns as they walked, two of them carrying the stretcher and one resting. Even so, they were tired and hungry, and they still had a long way to go. This was the kind of situation where psi could really be helpful. Taemon and Amma could have used psi to carry the stretcher with very little exertion. They might even have been able to press on through the night and arrive at the colony by midmorning.

Instead, exhaustion forced them to stop and rest. They sat down next to another abandoned quadrider. They'd passed several since leaving the asylum. The windshield of this one was smashed; the owner had probably had to break it to get out. Without psi to open the door, a person could easily get trapped inside a car.

Taemon wondered if the days of quadriders were over. Would people go back to horses and carts? Or would someone take the time to convert the quadriders to corn fuel? Drigg was the only person who knew how, and it took weeks to do just one conversion.

This would be a good one to convert. It reminded

Taemon of the quadrider Uncle Fierre used to own before he bought his unisphere. He'd let Taemon drive it once and made him promise not to tell Mam.

Mam. He should be looking after Mam, not daydreaming about quadriders.

Taemon checked on her again while Amma pulled out the food and drink pouches she'd found in the asylum.

"How's she doing?" Amma asked.

Taemon shrugged. "Same, though I worry she'll be cold now that it's dark. I wish we could have found a blanket for her."

"I know," Amma said. "But the blankets must have been the first thing people took from the asylum. We're lucky we managed to find food and drink."

He ran his hands through his hair. "It's my fault. I tripped. Skies, if something happens to her, I . . ."

"She's been through a lot," Amma said. "None of that is your fault."

Taemon looked up. It *was* his fault, he wanted to tell her. All of it. But he couldn't say that in front of Drigg. He would have to bear the weight of his decision secretly, because if word got out that he was to blame for the Fall . . .

"If anyone's to blame, it's Elder Naseph," Anna continued. "He's the one who started all this business of using psi for evil." As if adding an exclamation point, she slapped a mosquito on her arm. "We'll get her to the colony, and everything will be fine," Amma said. "You wait and see."

Taemon nodded. He appreciated the encouragement, but things had not been fine in a long, long time. He had a feeling that fine was a good way off.

Amma handed him a pouch with a picture of an apple on the label. He was fiddling with the cap, trying to figure out how it opened, when a cloud blocked the moonlight.

"Amma, can you help me with this?" he asked, holding out the bottle toward her.

"You're worse than a child," Amma teased, her hand brushing his as she felt for the pouch.

Taemon was glad for the cover of darkness, which hid his flushed cheeks. He wasn't sure if it was the teasing or the brush of her fingers, though, that embarrassed him.

Suddenly, a man's voice echoed in the darkness.

"Everybody stop right where you are."

Taemon looked up to see a figure stepping forward

from the shadows. A figure who had a bow with an arrow nocked and aimed right at him.

Slowly, Taemon raised both hands. "We mean no harm."

"Maybe you don't," said the man. "But maybe we do."

More archers stepped into view. It was hard to count them in the dark, but Taemon thought he could see at least six. Were there more? The surrounding trees would make it easy for them to hide.

For a moment, everything was silent except for the distant throbbing of cicadas.

The archers were a ragged, scrappy-looking group, some men, some women, with mismatched clothes, lean bodies, and wild looks in their eyes. The one aiming at Taemon had stringy hair that hung in waves around his narrow face.

"What're you doing on this road after dark?" said the archer.

Taemon swallowed. "My mother's hurt. We're taking her to get help."

"That's your mother?" The man jerked his head toward Mam, but his eyes never left Taemon.

"Yes," Taemon answered. "We have to get her to—"

"Well, ain't that interesting?" The man smiled eerily. "The boy came for his mam." The others chuckled dutifully. "Get up slowly, now. The big man can carry the lady. We're takin' you to see Free Will."

"Look, she's hurt," Taemon protested. "Just let us go. We won't bother you."

His words had no effect.

"Who's Free Will?" Amma asked as one of the archers gathered up the food.

The man's grin grew wider. "You'll know soon enough."

"Should we tie 'em up, Lervie?" another archer asked.

"Nah," said the man—Lervie, apparently. "They won't do anything that might injure the lady. Just use your arrows to keep 'em in line. Now get goin'!" He shouted that last part and motioned with a quick twitch of the arrow.

Unfortunately, Lervie was right: they had no choice but to follow. Taemon set his mind to finding a way out of this. If it were just him, he could chance doing something reckless, like charging the leader and hoping the others would be too surprised to stop him. But there was Mam to think about. And Drigg and Amma. Still, there had to be a way out of this.

Under the archer's watchful eye, Taemon rose to his feet and inched closer to the quadrider. Perhaps he could push it over and distract Lervie long enough for them to get away. But a quadrider must be immensely heavy—far too heavy for him to tip over on his own.

If only he still had psi! He could tip the quadrider over with ease. Or better yet, they could pile into the quadrider and tear out of these woods before the archers knew what was happening. And Mam would be at the colony and under the care of the healers in no time.

Stop it! Useless, stupid thoughts like that weren't going to help. He had to think of a plan that had at least a chance of working, even if it was slim.

Still, the urge to drive the quadrider and get the blazes out of there was overwhelming, and the image of the engine came unbidden to his mind—the gears, the springs, the coils that stored energy as the driver gradually released it to the transmission. Before he realized what he was doing, Taemon reached out for psi. As if he had it. As if it had never left him.

An automatic response, he thought. *Like trying to turn on the lights even when you know the power is out. A mindless attempt at the impossible.*

But the engine roared to life.

The noise startled him and everyone else. The archers momentarily lowered their arrows.

Taemon's mind was reeling. Had he actually started that engine? There was one way to find out. In his mind, Taemon held the image of the doors opening and gave the order: *Be it so.*

All four doors swung open.

How had he done that? He pondered the impossibility of it for an entire second before snapping into action. The archers reacted, too. They raised their bows, and Taemon used psi to deflect the arrows harmlessly into the trees. Amma and Drigg hustled Mam inside the quadrider and settled her into the backseat. Drigg climbed in beside her, and Amma took the passenger's seat.

Taemon flung himself into the front seat, closed the doors, and threw as much psi as he dared into the engine. The quadrider rocketed forward, tires squealing as it sped past the archers.

Drigg leaned forward in the backseat. "What happened back there? I'm not complaining, mind you, but I'd really like to know who's driving this thing and how."

"I'm driving," Taemon said, not daring to turn around.

"How in the Great Green Earth can you do that?" Amma shouted over the roaring of the wind through the broken windshield.

"I don't know! My psi is back. Is yours?"

Amma was one of the few people in the powerless colony to have had psi before the Fall, though it had been a carefully guarded secret. Her family had been in charge of protecting a hidden library; there would have been deadly consequences if it had fallen into the hands of the city dwellers. Unfortunately, that's exactly what happened. A stupid mistake on Taemon's part had led to Elder Naseph and Yens discovering the library, and the books had been looted.

Amma frowned in concentration. Taemon wondered what she was trying to move with her mind. Was it working?

She blew out a breath. "No. How is this happening? Did the adrenaline trigger your psi somehow?"

"I've never heard of adrenaline, but there's no mistaking the feel of psi," Taemon said. He was turning his head to see how far they'd gotten when pain burst like starfire in his left shoulder.

He cried out, and the engine sputtered.

"You okay?" Amma leaned forward. "Taemon, you're hurt!"

He looked down and saw an arrow lodged in his shoulder just next to the joint. Skies! What now?

THREE

Choosing requires not choosing. Every choice eliminates countless other choices that will never avail themselves again.

— THE WARRIOR'S SERENITY

The arrow had come from the front. Flame it all! There must have been more archers hiding in the trees. How many more were there?

Faster. He had to go faster. They'd just have to outdistance the archers. He locked away the pain and poured all the psi he could manage into the engine. The back tires fishtailed before finding traction and rocketing the quadrider forward.

"It doesn't look like it's bleeding too badly," Amma said.

Drigg's voice came from the backseat. "Can you get us to the colony?"

Taemon clenched his jaw. "I have to."

The engine faltered, and the car swerved. Taemon had to focus entirely on the quadrider to correct their course.

"We can talk later," Amma said to Drigg. "Right now he just needs to drive."

Taemon tried to ignore the pain in his shoulder and focus on his psionic connection with the engine.

Holy Mother Mountain, he had psi!

Why? How? Psi was gone. For everybody. The exact words he'd said were burned into his mind: "Let all psi in Deliverance be done away. Let each man and woman work by the power of his own hands."

Other words were spoken that day as well.

Skies, he knew that voice in his head! The Heart of the Earth was speaking to him again.

Let me help you remember.

Without his bidding, his memory flashed to a moment before the Fall. Taemon and Amma had been caught trying to expose Yens and Elder Naseph as false prophets, and Elder Naseph had just ordered Yens to kill them. Taemon, who had lost his psi months earlier and been banished to the powerless colony, had asked the Heart of the Earth to restore his psi so he could save himself and Amma and stop Yens and Elder Naseph from wielding their terrible psi weapons.

Once again, he heard the Heart of the Earth's response:

Consider carefully. You cannot request a gift only to discard it at will. If you ask me to restore your power, the restoration will be permanent.

Was that it? Had her warning meant that his psi hadn't gone away when he'd willed away the psi of others? Did he alone have psi?

The thought was chilling.

But how hadn't he noticed this before? Certainly life had been difficult for everyone, him included, since the Fall. Why hadn't his psi kicked in earlier, when he'd been so exhausted from rebuilding destroyed homes in the city or gathering and distributing food and supplies? Why hadn't he just moved the endless parade of heavy objects around with his mind and spared himself the blisters and cuts and bruises?

Then again, had he even tried to reach out for psi since the Fall? Had he even once tried to move something with telekinesis or see something with clairvoyance? No, he had assumed he was powerless, just like everyone else. Only tonight, when he'd felt threatened and desperate, had his mind longed for psi enough to reach for it.

His shoulder was stiffening up. He clenched his jaw and drove on.

He had psi. It should make him happy, he supposed. After all, it had gotten them out of that mess with that gang. And it meant getting Mam to the healers much sooner, for which he was grateful.

But the truth was, psi did not make him happy. It never had. He'd actually liked using his hands and feeling his muscles ache after a hard day's work. He also liked using touch to show affection, hugging his friends or holding hands with Amma. Da had always insisted that the family honor the Sabbath by not using psi on that day, which other families had scoffed at. But Da had said that doing so brought them closer to the Heart of the Earth, and when Taemon had become powerless, he'd finally understood what Da had meant by that.

But now he was the odd duck once again, the freakling, different from everyone else. Only this time he knew he would face something far worse than banishment if anyone found out.

The pain in his shoulder had changed from a burning fire to a crushing weight. The quadrider swerved, and the engine sputtered multiple times. About thirty minutes away from the colony, the pain became unbearable. Taemon was forced to pull off the road.

"I need to stop," Taemon panted. Drigg snored softly in the backseat. *At least someone is comfortable,* Taemon thought.

Amma looked at him with concern as she lifted a water pouch for him to drink. "What can I do?"

Skies, his shoulder hurt like blazes. "I have to do something about this pain. It's making it impossible to use psi. The arrow has to come out."

"Don't even think about doing that with psi," Amma said. "Let the healers do that. You can do a lot of damage if you try to use psi on yourself, Taemon. Even I know that. Besides, if the arrow nicked an artery, it might be safer to keep the arrow in place."

"I can't drive like this," Taemon said. "I'm not even sure I can walk."

"*I* can walk. I'll go get someone from the colony," Amma said. "We can come back for you with the farm hauler."

It wasn't a bad idea, but it would take time—a couple

of hours at least. And Mam might not have a couple of hours. By the look on Amma's face, he could tell that she knew it, too.

The arrow would have to come out. He was pretty sure he could remove it with psi; moving an arrow a couple of inches was a lot easier than operating a quadrider engine. But that bleeding part didn't sound so great.

"What's an artery?" Taemon asked.

Amma sighed. "I can't believe they didn't teach you these things. It's terrible not to understand your own body."

Lots of information had been kept from the city dwellers, especially the type that could be used to harm others—like human anatomy. If a psi wielder knew how to manipulate the inner workings of the human body, there would be no limit to the damage he could inflict on others. But in the powerless colony, even little kids knew how their bodies worked. There was no harm in that knowledge for them.

Taemon tensed and grunted as another wave of pain crashed over him. Then it subsided. "So teach me. What's an artery?"

"Arteries are the tubes inside your body that carry

blood from the heart to all the other places in your body. There's a big one right around your armpit somewhere."

Pushing the pain aside, Taemon tried to think. If he had psi, then he should be able to use clairvoyance to see what was happening inside his body. Taemon closed his eyes and sent his awareness toward his wounded shoulder. If he could find a way to remove the pain, they might have a chance at getting to the colony. He began with his heart, then followed the tubes that carried blood. They went everywhere, branching into smaller and smaller tubes. After a few wrong turns, he managed to follow the blood all the way to his shoulder. Amma was right: one of the bigger tubes went through his shoulder into his arm. But the arrow hadn't touched it.

"The artery's fine," he told Amma. "I'm going to use psi to pull out the arrow."

Amma frowned. "I really don't think that's a good idea."

"I won't be using psi on myself; I'll be using it on the arrow."

"Which is inside you. Same thing," Amma said. "I'll *run* to the colony. It will only take an hour."

Just then, Mam moaned from the backseat.

"That might not be fast enough," Taemon said, grimacing through his pain. "I have to try."

Amma gripped his hand, and Taemon felt a surge of strength from her touch that had nothing to do with psi.

He sat back. "Just give me a couple minutes. If it doesn't work, I'll need you to go for help."

She nodded gravely.

Using clairvoyance once more, he examined the arrow inside his shoulder. The arrowhead was a nasty piece of barbed metal, but the shaft was smooth and straight, so he started with that. He separated the wooden shaft from the arrowhead and slid it smoothly out of the wound. He was relieved to find that it didn't hurt at all. But when he released his psi, the pain came flooding back.

"Taemon?" Amma's voice was tinged with anxiety. "Are you okay?"

He nodded, but even that slight movement made him nauseated. "How's Mam doing?" he asked.

Amma craned her head to see into the backseat. "It's hard to say," she said. "She's still unconscious, but she looks a little paler, maybe."

"I'm not sure I can remove the arrowhead," he confessed. "If I try to drag it backward through the flesh, I could lose consciousness before I finish." Just saying the words made him light-headed.

"I wish we had some kind of pain medicine," Amma said. "Just enough to help you concentrate on driving."

"You're right," Taemon said. "The pain's the problem right now, not the arrowhead. If I can make it to the colony, the healers can take care of the rest."

"What do you mean? How do you plan to stop the pain without medicine?"

But Taemon wasn't listening. He sent his awareness deeper into his shoulder, and then all the way to his brain. He wasn't sure exactly what caused pain, besides the wound itself, but it must involve his brain somehow. There had to be something that triggered the effect, something that set off the blaring alarms that translated into pain. He couldn't say exactly what he was seeing in his shoulder and in his brain. He had no words for it. But when he thought he knew what to do, he used every last squinch of discipline to calm himself for one more burst of psi. After this, he would either stop the pain or pass out trying.

Holding the image of what he desired in his mind, he gave the command: *Be it so!*

And the pain was gone.

No, not just the pain, he realized. His shoulder was numb. It was an odd sensation, but infinitely better than the blinding pain.

He felt his body unclench and relax.

"What happened?" Amma asked. "I don't see the arrowhead."

"I had to leave it in there for now, but I figured out how to dull the pain."

Amma looked worried. "You really shouldn't do that. Nerves are very complex things, Taemon, and you could cause a lot of damage if you don't know what you're doing."

"Nothing the healers can't fix, I'm sure," he assured her. "At least I can drive. That's what's important."

Amma didn't look convinced, but another moan from Mam distracted her. "Let's get you both to the healers as quickly as possible."

About a mile away from the colony, Amma pointed to the side of the road. "Pull over and park the quadrider there. We can walk the rest of the way."

"What? Why?" Taemon asked. "That will take too long."

"It's a good idea," Drigg said, leaning forward and rubbing sleep from his eyes.

Amma looked pointedly at Taemon. "Think about it. How are we going to explain you driving this quadrider? I don't think you should tell people about your psi. Not unless you have a way to bring it back for everyone. . . ."

"No! I can't do that." The Heart of the Earth had made it clear his decision was permanent. But Amma was right. She was terribly right. People would despise the one person who still had psi. What would they do? Imprison him? *Execute* him?

"We can rest a while if you need to," Amma said. "Until you're ready to walk."

"I'm ready now." Taemon opened the doors with psi. "Mam needs a healer."

They arrived at the colony twenty minutes later, on foot. Drigg carried Mam, and Taemon tried to appear normal as he walked beside Amma. But the numbness in his shoulder was starting to worry him. He could barely feel the fingers on his left hand, and when he tried to make a fist, his fingers would curl only partway. What if Amma was right, and he had been foolish to mess with his nerves?

They headed straight to the healing house.

Urland, one of the healers, came out and met them. Taemon tried to explain about Mam, but suddenly realized that he was incredibly exhausted.

On the edge of consciousness, Taemon heard Amma explain who Mam was and what had happened to her, and about the arrow in Taemon's shoulder. His only goal now was to reach the bed at the far side of the room before he fell asleep.

He couldn't tell if he made it or not. All he knew is that when he woke up the next morning, his aunt, Challis, was in the room with him.

And she was crying.

FOUR

That which is impossible and that which is possible never changes. What changes is our conception of that which is possible.

— THE WARRIOR'S SERENITY

Challis was crying. Did that mean Mam was gone?

Taemon tried to reach forward and touch Challis, to comfort her somehow, but he found he couldn't lift his injured arm from the bed. "Is it Mam?" he asked, his voice barely a whisper. "Is she . . . ?"

"She's alive," said Challis. "She's still unconscious, but she's alive. She's in the next room."

Taemon held his aunt's gaze. There was something Challis wasn't telling him. "What else?"

Before the Fall, Challis used to have two very rare types of psi: precognition, which meant seeing things before they happened, and remote viewing, or seeing events that happened far away. Her visions of the future weren't always clear or easy to interpret, which had frustrated her and made her mix up the present and the past, but back then, just like now, Taemon constantly felt like she knew more than she was saying.

In the four months since the Fall, though, Challis seemed a bit more with it, as though losing her abilities had been a blessing rather than a curse, as others saw it.

Her gaze was clear and steady when she finally looked up at him.

"The healers don't know if she'll ever wake up."

"What do you mean they don't know? It's their job to know." The anger he heard in his own words surprised him. He wasn't sure where it had come from.

Challis shook her head. "There's no way to know."

"Ah, you're awake." Urland stood in the doorway. He turned to Challis. "Does he know about the extent of the damage yet?"

Challis hesitated. "No, he just now woke—"

"How bad is it?" Taemon tried to push himself up into a

sitting position, but his left elbow buckled and he lurched to one side.

Challis sprang forward to steady him. His shoulder no longer hurt, but it didn't seem to work very well, either.

"Just tell me what's wrong with Mam," Taemon said.

The healer frowned. "I'm afraid we're not entirely sure what's wrong with your mother. As long as she remains unconscious, we're quite limited in what tests we can run," he said. "I was talking about the damage to your shoulder. There's some nerve damage that I can't explain. I've never seen anything like it. It's almost as if . . ."

Urland's words were drowned out by voices from the hall.

Hannova, the leader of the colony, came into the small room, which was starting to feel crowded.

"I'm glad to see you're awake," she said. "You gave us quite a scare."

"I'm fine," Taemon assured her. He lifted his blanket with his good hand and swung his feet to the side of the bed. "But I'd like to go check on my mother."

Urland started to object, but Challis cut him short. "I'll take you to her," she said.

"Come see me in my office when you can," said Hannova. "I want to hear about what happened."

"He should be resting," Urland said.

"When you can," Hannova repeated, then left the room while Taemon, waving off assistance, hauled himself out of bed.

The homespun cotton tunic Taemon wore felt more than a little drafty as he padded down the hall. Luckily, he didn't have far to go.

As much as he wanted to see Mam, he held back just outside her door. *Unconscious. Might never wake up.* Surely someone could figure out how to help her. If not the doctors, then maybe *he* could heal her—or at least figure out what was wrong with her. Maybe that's why his psi had come back, so he could heal Mam. Da had always said psi was for helping people. With psi he could see what was going on inside her body just as he'd done with his shoulder wound.

And look how great that turned out, he thought, clutching his useless left arm.

Challis beckoned him, and Taemon walked in. A frail Mam lay in a bed identical to the one he'd just left. Her cheekbones stuck out, her eyelids looked gray, and her arms lay still as stone. But beneath the covers, her chest rose and fell. Mam was alive.

Taemon slid into the chair next to the bed and ran his hands along the wooden armrests. He felt like he should do something, but what? Challis's hand squeezed his shoulder. He turned to look at her and noticed that she had a hand on each of his shoulders. But he could only feel it on his good side.

"Talk to her," Challis said.

"Can she hear me?"

"It's possible. But maybe it doesn't matter. Maybe you just need to talk."

Emotions tossed and tumbled inside him. Sadness. Anger. Regret. And something more, something he couldn't name. Maybe there was no word for it. Maybe no one had ever felt it before.

"I'm sorry," he whispered to Mam. "It was my fault you were sent to the asylum. My fault they took Da away. And it's my fault people are starving. It's all my fault, Mam. All of it!"

Calming his thoughts, he touched his mother's hand and studied her face. Not a twitch. Not a flutter.

He closed his eyes and let his clairvoyance flow into

Mam. Her heart was beating, blood circulating, lungs breathing, but there was little else. His awareness drifted into her brain. He had so little knowledge of what was supposed to happen there. But something was definitely wrong, very wrong. It was so complicated, so complex—

"Don't." Someone gripped his right shoulder forcefully.

Taemon released his psi and turned to see Challis peering at him. "How did you know—?"

"Amma told me what happened. But don't." She motioned with her eyes to the doorway, and Taemon saw Urland lingering there. He wasn't sure how Challis knew that he'd been using psi just then, but he hoped that Urland hadn't noticed, too.

The healer walked into Mam's room.

"She hit her head pretty hard when she fell on the sidewalk," Taemon said. "Is that what caused . . . ?" He couldn't bring himself to finish the sentence.

Urland looked at him and then at Challis. "I'm not sure how much you know about the asylums, but they were not good. The drugs the patients were given to suppress their psionic ability were brutal on the brain functions. It could be that your mother will wake up and fully recover.

Or she might have permanent brain damage, the extent of which we won't know until she wakes."

"So you think she'll wake up?" Taemon tried to focus on that rather than on the words "permanent brain damage."

Urland frowned. "I'm afraid there's just no way to know."

Taemon took a deep breath and let it out slowly. "Can we have some time alone with her?"

When the healer left the room, Taemon turned to Challis. "Do you know what's going to happen to her? Did your precognition tell you anything before the Fall? Anything about Mam?"

Challis shook her head sadly. "I see bits and pieces of the future. I mean, saw. And I didn't get to pick the things I saw. But I don't have that power anymore, Taemon, and I'm glad of it. It's a burden I can do without."

It was still a bit odd to hear Challis call him by his real name. He'd gotten used to her calling him Thayer back before the Fall.

Challis settled into the other chair in the room. "Amma mentioned that your mam was raving when you found her—talking to the mops and brooms and muttering about the pills she was taking."

Taemon nodded. " 'Two yellow. One blue. Three red.' "

"Did she say anything else to you before she lost consciousness? Anything that could be important—no matter how crazy it might have seemed?"

Taemon shook his head, thinking she was asking for medical reasons. But then he remembered: Mam *had* said something important!

Taemon opened his mouth to tell her but hesitated.

"Go on," Challis urged. "What is it?"

He glanced at the doorway to make sure they were alone. "She also said . . . She said that they had taken Da to the Republik."

"The Republik? That can't be right."

"Mam said I should go find him," Taemon said.

"She wasn't in her right mind, Taemon," Challis warned. "She never would have suggested such a thing if she was. You'd do best to get that idea out of your head."

Taemon knew better than to argue. But if there was a chance—however small—that his da was still alive and needed his help, how could he just forget about that?

"Besides," said Challis, settling back into her chair, "how could you even hope to do that? No one's made it across those mountains and lived to tell of it."

No one yet, thought Taemon.

Later, back in his room, Taemon ate the meal Urland had brought him and thought about what Mam had said.

The Republik. Why would Da be there? And how could he have made it over Mount Deliverance? Three hundred years earlier, when the prophet Nathan had brought his people here, he'd made sure they would be safe from the rest of the world. He'd used psi to pull up the ridge of mountains that cradled the city of Deliverance against the coast. But it wasn't just the mountains that kept Deliverance separate from the Republik. There was also superstition and fear and a kind of pride in being set apart from the rest of the world. In some ways, these feelings made a stronger barrier than the mountains.

Da must have been taken there against his will. Taemon could think of no other explanation. "They took him. They took darling away." Isn't that what Mam had said? So someone in the Republik wanted Da. Why?

Just before the Fall, Elder Naseph had been talking

about forging an alliance with the Republik and making psi weapons for them to use in a war they were fighting. Against whom? Taemon wondered. Was it a civil war or a war with another nation? There was so much Taemon didn't understand, and there was no one to ask. The one thing Yens had said before he died was that he was going to be the one to trigger the weapons, since the Republikites were all powerless. That was why Taemon had decided to get rid of psi altogether—to prevent his brother and Naseph from using psi to commit unspeakable atrocities. But now psi was gone and Yens was dead. So what could the Republik want with a powerless man from the city?

But would the Republikites know that Deliverance was now powerless? News of the Republik never reached the people of Deliverance, so it was safe to assume that news of Deliverance didn't reach the Republik. If the Republikites still believed the people of the city had psi, what would they make of Yens's no-show? Would they think that Naseph had betrayed them?

Taemon's mind spun. If the weapons were already in place in the Republik, would they have sent someone over Mount Deliverance to find a replacement trigger? It still didn't explain how they'd selected Da, but perhaps it was a simple case of being in the wrong place at the wrong time.

If that was true—if they'd kidnapped Da to get him to operate their psi weapons—then what would happen to Da when they found out all the psi weapons were useless?

Skies, could any of this be true, or was Taemon as crazy as Mam? He needed to talk to someone about this. Someone who he knew was thinking clearly.

Taemon dressed himself (more slowly than he would have liked, thanks to his injured shoulder) and headed for Hannova's office. It was time to let someone with authority know what was going on.

As he stood in front of Hannova's office, Taemon started to reach out for psi to open the door but caught himself just in time. Strange how quickly those old psionic habits came back! Anyway, using psi to turn a doorknob was just foolish. Doorknobs were for people who didn't have psi. A psi latch would be inside the door, where it didn't show.

Using psi was wrong for bigger reasons, too. Everyone

else in the colony was powerless. For that matter, every-one else in the *world* was powerless. It seemed rude to use psi, like eating the only piece of cake while all your friends watched.

Skies! He was standing in front of the door, staring at it like a freakling. *Just open the flaming door and stop thinking about every blasted thing!*

He pushed the door open by hand. About a dozen of the colony's leaders were sitting in Hannova's office.

"I'm telling you, that quadrider was not there before." That was Mr. Parvel, Amma's da, who seemed steamed up about something. He used to be in charge of guarding the library. Now he and Amma's grown-up brothers were in charge of guarding the whole town.

Hannova turned to Taemon. "Hello, Taemon. It's good to see you up and about. Is there something we can help you with?"

Taemon swallowed. He hadn't expected to confess his fears in front of such a large audience. "You said to come see you when I could," he reminded her.

"So I did," Hannova agreed, nodding. "I was hoping you could tell us about these thieves led by someone called Free Will. This isn't the first time they've accosted travelers. Could they have something to do with the mysterious new quadrider?"

"It's been months since any psi vehicle has moved," Mr. Parvel jumped in. "And all of a sudden there's a new one on the side of the road? Why am I the only one who thinks that's a problem?"

"I'll agree that it's suspicious," Hannova said. "But there must be a simple explanation."

"Only one thing can move a psi vehicle: psi," Mr. Parvel said. "If Free Will's people have psi, we're all doomed."

"Now, now," Hannova cautioned, raising her hand to quiet the nervous chatter that had erupted at Amma's da's words. "Let's not jump to any hasty conclusions. Aside from the mysterious appearance of this quadrider, there is no evidence to suggest that anyone has psi."

Taemon caught Drigg's eye across the room. Should he confess and put an end to the wild speculation before it erupted into full-on panic?

"I know how the quadrider got there," Taemon said. The room fell silent as everyone stopped to listen to him. "When Free Will's men had us, I—"

"They carried it," Drigg said, cutting him off.

Hannova frowned. "What's that, Drigg?"

"Free Will's people. The ones who chased us here, the ones who shot the boy. We saw them carry the quadrider. Maybe they meant to take it back to their headquarters, wherever that is, and try to turn it into something useful—I don't know. But we startled a group of 'em, and they left it behind. That's how the quadrider came to be there. Simple as that."

"Why didn't you say so before?" Mr. Parvel asked, looking more than a little embarrassed.

"Didn't seem important," Drigg muttered. "Not when we've got real problems to deal with."

"Drigg's right," Hannova said. "There are some very disturbing rumors floating around, and I want to know if there's any truth to them. Solovar has the best connections with the city, so I'll let him fill you all in."

Solovar was the white-bearded leader of the city dwellers; he had tried to rebel against Elder Naseph. Now that Naseph was out of the way, Solovar could move freely throughout the city and make good use of his networks of former spies.

Solovar cleared his throat and spoke in his gravelly voice. "Things in the city are getting worse. People are still hoping to find a way to get psi back. They're getting desperate. The thought of rebuilding the things that keep society running—the power plant, the quadriders, the elevators, the doors, the locks, the plumbing—that's overwhelming. Getting psi back seems like a better option to them."

"But that's not possible," Taemon said, shifting uncomfortably in his seat.

Solovar leaned forward in his chair. "Yes, but they won't accept that. And here's the trouble: there are people in the city who claim to have a plan to return psionic powers to the people. They're asking for donations, making promises, and showing their progress by giving street demonstrations, which are nothing more than tricks."

Taemon looked down at his hands. That was the kind of thing he used to do back when he had to pretend to have psi. Lies, deception, trickery. "Those tricks won't fool people for long," Taemon said. "I wouldn't worry too much about the charlatans."

"You have to understand," Solovar said. "People are scared. There are all kinds of wild tales spreading."

"Like what?" Drigg asked.

"Like innocents still alive and trapped in secret underground chambers at the temple. Like people crossing

Mount Deliverance to make contact with the Republik. There's even a story about a ghost haunting one of the churches."

Drigg laughed, which made Solovar's scowl even deeper. "It may sound like rubbish to you and me. But there are people out there who are so desperate, they'll believe anything."

"What if they're right?" Taemon whispered.

Solovar looked confused. "You really think there's a ghost in the —?"

"Of course not. But the rumor about people crossing the mountain. My mam said something about that, too. She said that Da was in the Republik and that I should go find him."

"Your mam wasn't in her right mind," Hannova said gently. "Amma told us how she was when you found her. She was probably just repeating some nonsense she'd overheard."

"Besides," Solovar added, "no one can cross those mountains. It's impossible."

Amma's father cleared his throat. "Actually, that's not quite true."

All eyes turned to him. "What are you saying, Birch?" Hannova asked.

"There were documents in the library. I can't be sure, mind you. They were very old and cryptic. But the way I interpret them, I think . . ."

Hannova slapped both hands on her desk. "For Skies' sake! Out with it!"

"I think there's a way to cross Mount Deliverance."

FIVE

It's not the trap that is dangerous, but the deception.

— THE WARRIOR'S SERENITY

"A way over Mount Deliverance?" Hannova said. "Are you sure?"

"No. In fact, I'm very unsure," Mr. Parvel said. "But there was a map in the library that makes me think there is a way. Or was at one time. But I never studied the map closely. My grandfather gave me strict instructions to keep it secret, and I thought the less I knew about it, the better."

Hannova drummed her fingers on her desk, looking like she was thinking a million things at once. "You might have mentioned this when Elder Naseph took everything from the library. If the Republik has that map . . ."

Mr. Parvel stiffened defensively. "I didn't see any reason to bring it up until now. For all we know, everything from the library is buried under the rubble of the temple. Even if all the documents survived, it would take someone months to go through everything."

"So it *is* possible," Taemon said, his pulse quickening.

"Not without the map," Mr. Parvel added quickly. "Assuming it was even accurate."

"And even if we had the map," Hannova broke in, holding Taemon's gaze, "we couldn't allow a thirteen-year-old boy to attempt to cross the mountains and enter enemy territory."

"But no one would suspect a kid," Taemon said. *Especially a kid with psi,* he thought but couldn't very well say. "Besides, it's my da. If anyone should risk the trip, it should be me."

Arguing broke out among the adults. While Hannova could see the value in knowing more about the Republik, she didn't think it was safe for anyone—and certainly not Taemon—to attempt the trip alone. Drigg volunteered to go, but Solovar pointed out that the work of converting another hauler was more important than some "fool's errand."

Mr. Parvel spoke up. "Just because crossing the mountain might be possible doesn't mean it's a good idea. This late into autumn, there could be snowfall on the mountains soon. Anyone caught in a storm at this time of year would surely die."

But Taemon didn't much care what anyone else thought. If there was a way over Mount Deliverance, he was going to find it. His father needed him. And Mam would need Da when she woke up.

Taemon stood up. "I think I'm going to go back to my room now. Get some rest."

Hannova nodded. "We shouldn't have kept you so long. We can talk again in the morning."

Taemon headed for the door. He wasn't about to go take a nap. Not when he needed to prepare for his trip to the Republik.

He nearly ran into Amma, who was standing outside the door, just out of the line of sight. She followed him back to his room.

"Why do I get the feeling you're not just here to check in on me?" he asked eventually, suspicious of her silence.

"I'm going, too," she blurted. "I can help."

"Going where?"

"To the Republik!" She looked around, then lowered her voice: "To the Republik. You can't go alone—and don't even try to tell me that you're not planning on going. I know you too well, Taemon Houser."

"You heard all of that?" he whispered. "What we were saying in Hannova's office?"

"I couldn't help it," Amma said. "They were plenty loud. Urland asked me to find you and send you back to bed. But I can tell that's not going to happen."

Part of him wanted Amma to come with him. But it was the selfish part of him. The last time she'd gone with him, she could have easily been killed along with Moke.

Moke. Taemon didn't dare let his mind linger too long on that sadness. He didn't think he could bear having another friend's death on his conscience.

"It's going to be hard to cross the mountains this time of year," he said. "We could get lost. We could freeze or starve or worse. And once we get to the Republik, there's no telling what we'll be up against. You should stay. There's plenty you can do here to help. You could even watch over Mam, be there to explain everything to her when she wakes up."

"Challis will do that," Amma said. "It would mean a lot more to your mam than some strange girl trying to tell her what's happened to her son and her husband.

"Besides," Amma continued, "if you want to cross the mountain, you need me."

Taemon frowned. "What do you mean?" He looked around and whispered, "I'm the one with psi. What can you—?"

"I've seen the map, Taemon. I know the way."

Taemon froze. "You have? I thought it was top secret. Not even your da looked at it!"

Amma looked guilty. "I wasn't supposed to look at it, either. My da had told my oldest brother and me about it, how important it was, how *secret* it was. I was pretty young at the time—too young to understand why anything in the library should be kept a secret from us. Our whole lives were supposed to be devoted to guarding the library and all its secrets. Why would we ever tell anyone about anything we saw, including some dumb map? So one night I snuck into the library, found the map, and memorized it. I'm not proud of it, but right now it makes me pretty valuable to you, I'd say."

Taemon shook his head. "Your father will have a fit if you come with me."

"I don't plan on seeking his permission," Amma said with a determined air.

Taemon knew when he'd been beaten. "Fine. But you can't tell *anyone*."

"Of course not."

"Gather what supplies you can tomorrow. We'll set out at dawn two days from now."

That night, Taemon was back in his old room next to Drigg's workshop, having promised Urland that he would take it easy. It was late, but as much as he tried to sleep, tried to let the thrumming of the cicadas clear his mind, it wasn't working. His problems seemed suffocating. He got up and went into the workshop. Drigg, who was asleep upstairs, had laid out parts of an engine he was working on. Taemon looked over the parts; he didn't need clairvoyance to see how they would all come together in one harmonious machine. Why couldn't life be like that? Nothing ever seemed to fit together or work the way it was supposed to.

The sound of the front door opening startled him. Challis came in and sat down on the bench.

"Saw the light on in here, and I thought we should talk. I have something for you." She placed a scarf in his hands. It was blue and green and yellow, with some orange and brown and a strand of silver that meandered throughout. When he held it up, he thought he saw an image of some sort, but as soon as he tried to make sense of it, it vanished into randomness. Challis's scarves had always been fairly . . . unusual.

"I made it months ago," Challis said. "Before the Fall. Never got around to giving it to you."

He wondered why she felt the need to give it to him now. If this were the pre-Fall days, he would wonder if she knew about his plans. But the timing had to be coincidental—if odd.

"Thanks. I don't have a scarf."

"Amma will like it," Challis said.

That sounded like the old Auntie Challis, the one who knew things before they happened. Taemon peered at her.

"Did you see that? Do you know anything about what's going to happen next?"

Challis waved her hand dismissively. "Skies, no. I don't need precognition to know that Amma likes bright colors."

He looked at his aunt, wondering if she was being truthful with him. But then he was hardly being truthful with her.

She nodded at the scarf. "I didn't just come by to give you that. I want to know more about you getting your psi back."

So there *was* an ulterior motive to Challis's visit. Taemon played with the ends of the scarf as he talked. "I didn't have it when I was in the colony," he said, needing to clarify that point. "And I didn't have it when we got caught and then escaped from the prison. When Moke—" He wasn't ready to talk about Moke. If only he'd had psi when Moke had been injured! He could have fixed him— he could have *saved* him—instead of watching him die.

He cleared his throat. "But when Yens captured Amma and me, I spoke to the Heart of the Earth and asked her to return my psi to me. It was the only way to save Amma.

Yens was going to kill her." He looked straight at Challis. "And he was going to kill me, too. I knew that if I had psi, I could stop him."

Challis nodded, and he knew she didn't judge him for his actions—or for where those actions had led.

"And then you asked the Heart of the Earth to do away with everyone's psi but your own?" she said.

"No!" Taemon protested. "I mean, I *did* ask her to get rid of psi, but for *everyone*. Me included. I just didn't realize that when I asked her to give me my psi back, it would be forever."

"And you just now figured out that you still have psi?" Challis said. Was there a hint of doubt in her voice? "It's been months since that day."

"I never tried to use it. Not till we were in real trouble, surrounded by those archers. Even then I didn't expect it to actually *work*."

Challis replied with a *hmph*.

Taemon blushed, as though he'd been caught in a lie. "I don't intend to use psi very much," Taemon said. "Only when I absolutely have to, like to get away from Free Will's men or stop the pain in my shoulder so I could drive back to the colony."

"Which brings me to my next question." She frowned and poked his left shoulder. "What's going on with this?"

It should have hurt, the way she jabbed him like that. But if he hadn't seen her do it, he wouldn't even have known she'd touched him.

"I don't know. I guess it just needs time to heal."

Challis gave him a worried look. "I heard Urland discussing your shoulder with the other healers. They were talking about the signs of a psi wound."

"A psi wound? What's that?" He hoped he didn't sound as guilty as he felt.

"Psi is tricky to begin with," Challis explained, "and using it on yourself becomes even more complicated. There are so many things at work when you use psi: authority, knowledge, energy, intent. And the interplay of emotions and psi is especially complicated. If you use psi at a time when you are experiencing strong emotions, your psi can become bonded with the object you are influencing. For example, when psiball players have a strong desire to win, that desire can meld with the psi they're directing at the ball, making it more accurate so that they score more goals. And if your mam is feeling especially kindly toward you when she's cooking your favorite meal, that love works its way into the food.

"But if you're experiencing strong *negative* emotions—like fear or pain or hatred—and if the object you're acting on is your own body, then your psi works against your body, damaging it or attacking it."

"You're saying my psi is now attacking my shoulder, even though I used it to heal myself? That doesn't make any sense."

"There are many things about psi that you don't understand—that no one does. That's why it's so dangerous—and foolish—to use psi on yourself," she added pointedly.

"I told the healers that the psi aspect of your wound could be a holdover from your accident in the sea cave, before you came to the colony," she continued, "but I'm not sure they believed me. And if Free Will's men start talking about a boy who drove a quadrider, then it won't be long before suspicions turn to you. I think it might be a good idea for you to lie low for a while. Maybe stay with Bynon on the farm until things die down."

Skies, he hadn't thought about Free Will's men telling stories. With rumors of the return of psi already circulating in the city, talk like that could add fuel to the fire.

"You're very talented," Challis said. "You can do incredible things with psi, but you have to be careful. You may not always understand the consequences of your actions."

"I don't even want to use psi at all," Taemon said. "It seems unfair, like I'm cheating by having it."

"You're the True Son," Challis said. "Without psi, you can't do what you need to do."

"Haven't I already done it?" Taemon whispered. Stopping Naseph and Yens. Getting rid of psi. Hadn't that fulfilled his obligation as True Son?

Challis gave him a solemn look. "Not even close."

The next morning, Taemon got up before dawn, even though he'd gotten only a few hours' sleep. He intended to be on his way before the sun came up, one day earlier than what he'd told Amma. He hated lying, but he hated the thought of putting her in danger even more.

The night before, he'd collected a week's worth of food. Assuming he could find the path over the mountain without too much difficulty, that should be plenty. And he could always supplement with berries, roots, and small game if it came to that.

He'd needed a few other supplies, too, and he figured that the workshop would be a good place to scavenge a few useful items.

But Drigg had beaten Taemon to it. He was already there, rummaging through drawers, pulling out tools. A knife. A flashlight. A tinderbox. Drigg paused and stared at Taemon for a moment, then busied himself with coiling a rope.

"Saw all the food you had piled in your room. Figured you'd be leaving today," Drigg said gruffly. "Won't pretend I like this idea. I hate it. But I can see you're fixed on it."

"I am," Taemon said. "I have to find my da."

Drigg scowled, wrapped the end of the rope around the coil, and tied it with a vengeance. "It just doesn't sit right with me, a lad crossing the mountains on his own. I know I'm not your da, but you're my apprentice, and that carries some responsibility. I wish this could wait until spring. I could go with you then."

"You're needed here," Taemon said. "Like Solovar said, we need another hauler more than we need to rescue my da."

Drigg frowned. "You know he didn't mean it like that. It's just there's no guarantee your da's even in the Republik. And how under the blazing sun are you going to find the way over them mountains? Have you thought about that?"

"I'll have to use psi," Taemon said.

"Psi," Drigg scoffed. "Psi don't tell you where the gap in the mountains is. If there is one. Psi don't fill your belly. And psi don't keep you warm and dry when a blizzard shows up."

Actually, psi could do all of that—or at least Taemon's psi could. Psi could help him trap small animals for food, and it could tell him where the gap was. And if it started to snow, psi could help him build a fire and erect a shelter. But Drigg didn't know about Taemon's clairvoyance, about how Taemon could send his mind outside himself to explore the world. Even for a psi wielder, this was a peculiar ability. But now was not the time to go into all that. Besides, Drigg had been powerless his whole life; he was always going to be suspicious of psi.

"I'm going," Taemon said. There was nothing more to say.

"I know, I know," Drigg said. "You've set your mind

on it. I don't expect to sway you. But you're taking these things with you."

Drigg held the rope out. Taemon took it with his left hand, but he fumbled and nearly dropped it.

Drigg frowned.

"That's my bad arm," Taemon said. "It'll get better."

"You come back in one piece, you hear?" Drigg said, his voice gravelly.

"I will," Taemon promised. And he almost believed it.

He left in the grayness before dawn. He wished there were a way to say good-bye to Amma, but he knew she was determined to come along. She would reason with him, maybe even persuade him. Amma's birth sign was Water, and water finds its way through fissures and cracks. He couldn't afford that. He'd put her in danger too many times already. He set out alone and told himself it was better that way. He was a Knife, he reminded himself. He would cut his own path.

The first step was to head toward the mountains, which was easy enough. When he got closer, he'd have to use clairvoyance to try to find a way through. Using psi to navigate was something he'd never done before, and practicing on this easy stretch of the journey seemed like a good idea.

As he walked on the dirt path, he let his feet settle into a comfortable cadence, let the rhythm of his steps lull his mind into a trance. Each step was a connection to the earth, a union with the soil, the rock below it, the grass around it, the air above it. His body was a small portion of a thriving, intelligent planet, a vessel for his conscious thoughts and desires, but he was not bound by that small vessel. He sent his consciousness out into his surroundings, extending his awareness. He perceived earthworms tunneling, flowers releasing pollen, an owl returning to its nest, roots stretching, deer foraging. So many things were happening at once that it almost overwhelmed him.

Tuning out everything else, he focused on the surface of the soil, where land met air. The rise and fall of it, the ridges and ruts. How far could he extend his awareness? He pushed outward, farther and farther. Things got fuzzy outside a radius of a mile or so. He ignored what was behind him and sent his awareness in a forward direction only. He could see much farther now—nearly two miles!

When he felt his perception weaken, he released his psi

and took a break. His head hurt, and the numbness in his shoulder seemed worse. This wasn't something a person could do continually. He'd need to be smart about conserving his energy. This psionic navigation took a particular kind of mental discipline, but he was certain that with practice, he could improve.

The path became narrower and narrower until it disappeared altogether. The incline was getting steeper, and the trees were becoming denser. He was nearing the foot of the mountain. He'd skip breakfast, go a little farther, and stop later for some lunch. He tried to relax and settle into a steady rhythm.

By ten thirty, Taemon could no longer ignore his rumbling stomach. Besides that, he was exhausted. He wasn't used to this much exertion—and he *was* still recovering from an injury.

He sat under a shady tree and slipped his knapsack off. Even though he was used to the powerless zippers and their little pull tabs, the fingers on his left hand did not seem to want to grip. He tried with his good hand, but even that was difficult. He stopped and tried to calm himself. He could do this. He just needed to relax.

He tried again with his right hand and made only a little progress. But he made enough space to stick his whole hand through it and force the zipper open with the pressure from his arm.

He managed to grab his water bottle but had trouble opening the cap. Skies, he was so clumsy! His entire left arm was numb and nearly useless, and his right arm was tingly and sluggish. He needed at least one good arm if he was going to make it across the mountain! Later, he'd have to climb rocks, grab the rope, and who knew what else.

Had using psi made his nerve damage worse? Was that how psi wounds worked? He wished he'd asked Challis more about that. If using psi made him weaker, what chance did he have of making it across this mountain on his own? Maybe he should turn back. Maybe Hannova and Drigg and all the others were right about the dangers of this trip.

A noise. A rustling noise. Footsteps, maybe. Was it an animal or a person? It was too far away to tell.

Who would be out here in the woods? Only one answer came to him: Free Will's band. He remembered Hannova saying that they made a habit of accosting travelers. He'd assumed she'd meant travelers on the road. But what if he'd been wrong?

Skies, if they found him like this, barely able to work a zipper, he would stand no chance of getting away. He had almost no psi to draw on right now, having wasted all his energy testing the reaches of his awareness.

Taemon crawled behind the tree and into the brush. He grabbed a stick with his right hand and used it to scatter leaves over the marks in the dirt that his movement had created. He willed himself to relax, to slow his breathing, to be still.

He heard it again. Definitely footsteps. Definitely human. And *running* now. Someone was following him. Several someones. In just a few seconds, they would come around the bend in the path into his line of sight. He crouched as low as he could, till he could just see over the brush.

Five. There were five. Two he recognized from the encounter a couple of days earlier. They were Free Will's men, no doubt about it. They stopped several yards before they reached the place where Taemon was hiding. Had they heard something? Did they know where he was?

They started talking, too quietly for him to hear them.

But they weren't looking his way. One of the men pointed into the forest across from where Taemon hid. Another got out a wire and strung it low across the forest floor, using trees as anchors. It was nearly invisible. Whatever—or whoever—they were tracking was going to trip over that wire. It was an ambush.

Free Will's men disappeared into the trees, probably to flush out their prey and drive it toward the wire. Were they setting up the trap for *him*? Had they spotted him earlier? Or were they after anyone they could find in the woods?

More rustling noises came from the trees. More of Free Will's men, or their intended victim?

"Taemon?" a familiar voice whispered. "Is that you?"

Breaking through the trees—and heading straight for the wire—was Amma.

SIX

Every soul learns to deal with adversity. Power is the true
test of integrity.

— THE WARRIOR'S SERENITY

There was no time even to think. Amma would be at the
wire in a second or two. He stared at the wire and envi-
sioned it snapping in half. *Be it so!*

The wire broke and recoiled violently against the trees.
Amma froze in shock. Free Will's men came charging
out of their hiding places, but still Amma stood there.
Why wasn't she moving? Free Will's men were almost
to her!

Taemon used psi to whip one end of the wire toward
the men, lashing the legs of the man closest to Amma.

The man cried out and fell to the ground, but his companions kept advancing. Taemon turned his attention to them, lashing them with the wire until each of them collapsed.

As the last man fell, Taemon's vision became blurry and turned dark around the edges. He looked around for Amma but couldn't see her—couldn't see much of anything. Had she gotten away?

He tried to lift himself up on his elbows but found that he couldn't move his arms. Tried to call out to Amma, but no sound came from his mouth.

All was quiet as Taemon lay in his hiding spot, trying to regain his strength. He'd wait a few minutes, then he'd try to find Amma. He hoped she'd gotten away.

He hadn't realized he'd fallen asleep until the whine of a mosquito woke him. The ground felt rough under his cheek. Pebbles, leaves, dirt. Why in the Great Green Earth was he sleeping outside? He hated camping.

Grunting, he turned over on his back. His mouth was painfully dry.

"Taemon?" a voice called from nearby.

It was Amma.

Then he remembered. The mountain. Free Will's men. The ambush attempt.

"I'm here," Taemon croaked. He hauled himself into a sitting position.

"There you are!" Amma rushed over to where he leaned against the tree. "I've been looking everywhere for you! It was you who saved me from Free Will's men, wasn't it? Are you okay? You look awful!"

"I'm fine," he lied, sitting up a bit straighter. "Free Will's men? Are they—?"

"They're gone. I ran ahead, then waited for them to clear out. I figured it was you who broke the wire and attacked them, so I knew you had to be close by. After they left, I started looking for you."

Taemon tried to stand up, but a wave of dizziness crashed over him and he slid back down the tree. He hung his head until the feeling subsided.

"What's wrong?" Amma asked.

Taemon rubbed his temples. "I think using psi made me weaker, somehow."

Amma frowned. "That doesn't sound good. Is it related to your shoulder injury, do you think? How are you feeling now?"

"Better. I just have to be careful. Learn my limits."

Amma frowned. "Will you admit now that you need me? You can't possibly make it over Mount Deliverance by yourself—not when using psi weakens you this much."

As much as Taemon hated to say it, Amma was right. If he had any hope of finding Da, he needed help. He needed Amma.

"Are you sure you remember the way?" Taemon asked, slowly getting to his feet. "You were only a kid when you saw the map."

Amma seemed to consider the question. "I'm pretty sure I remember everything. But if we get in a real bind, you can always use clairvoyance to see what's ahead. Between the two of us, we just might make it."

Taemon gathered up his supplies and pulled on his backpack. "Are you sure about this, Amma? I have to go. It's my da who's out there. But you—"

"Hey," Amma said, cutting him off. "We're in this together. We need each other. Besides," she said, picking her way through the brush, back toward the mountain, "if there's even the slightest chance that the books from my library ended up in the Republik . . . well, I can't very well just leave them in the hands of the enemy, can I?"

"Hannova thinks they're buried under the temple," Taemon said.

"But she can't know for sure. None of us can, at least not until all the rubble is finally cleared, which could take months. Since you're so all-fire determined to pay a little visit to the Republik now, I figure I might as well tag along and see if I can find out anything about the books."

"Do you really think that's likely?" Taemon asked. How in the Great Green Earth would someone carry that many books across the mountain? Or was Amma just using the books as an excuse to help him?

Amma had a distant look in her eyes. "This is all connected somehow. Elder Naseph was planning to use the books as leverage to make sure the Republik kept its side of the alliance. Even if the books are buried in the rubble of the temple, I'd like to know why they were so valuable to the Republik. It's still my family's responsibility to safeguard those books and whatever secrets they hold."

Taemon wondered if he should tell Amma what he thought was going on — that someone from the Republik had kidnapped Da to power its psi weapons. If that was true—if the Republik was still planning to go ahead with its war and was on the brink of discovering that the city of Deliverance was powerless—then Amma's books were now more dangerous than ever.

"All right," Taemon said. "Let's go."

SEVEN

Like a trickle becomes a mighty river, small acts accomplish great things.

— THE WARRIOR'S SERENITY

Seven days later, Taemon wondered if Amma was still glad she'd come along. Using her memory of the map, she had led them high into the mountains, and though the snow hadn't fallen yet, the nights were cold. The sweaters and camping blankets they'd brought weren't enough, but wood was scarce at this elevation, which meant they could build only small fires—barely big enough for preparing their meals, let alone warming their bodies.

Water, too, was a constant concern. They'd long since finished the water they'd brought, and the only streams they'd passed were shallow and muddy, hardly good for drinking. And in order to boil water to make it drinkable, they'd have to find more wood. It was a vicious cycle. Skies, even finding a place to go to the bathroom was an ordeal.

As for their food supply, it was holding out, but just barely. Soon they'd need to start supplementing it with food they could find on the mountain. This part of the journey involved hiking all day, every day. That was hard enough, but the difficult part was yet to come. Soon they would have to turn deeper into the rocky canyons and find the pass that would lead them to the Republik. They would need all the strength they could get.

They made camp for the night, and it was Amma's turn to build the fire. Taemon had learned enough from Amma to make a decent fire, but she was still much better at it than he was—especially with his injury. Taemon rummaged through his knapsack for something to make a meager meal, but he couldn't find anything. All their food was gone! His water bottle was missing, too. All the lightweight supplies were there—blankets, rope, twine, and Challis's scarf. But no food.

Taemon opened his mouth to shout to Amma and tell

her that their food was missing. Then it dawned on him. He checked Amma's knapsack. Sure enough, it was full of food, water, and the heaviest of the tools and supplies that Drigg had given him.

Amma had been trying to lighten his pack.

Quickly, while Amma was busy with the fire, Taemon redistributed the food and supplies so that the packs were equally heavy. His left arm may not be fully functioning, but until he needed to use psi to get them out of a tight spot, he was fully capable of pulling his own weight on this trip.

He put together a meal of dried fruit, travel bars, and jerky. "We're running pretty low on food," he said as he handed Amma her share.

"No problem," Amma said. "We can catch some of those ground squirrels we've been seeing."

Taemon cringed. "Squirrel meat?"

"It's not terrible. We had to eat it one year when most of the cattle died. And it cooks up pretty quick, so no need for big fires."

"I suppose I could use a little psi to trap them."

"No," Amma said. "I know how to set a snare. We'll save your psi till we really need it — *if* we really need it."

"If I'm careful, if I use just a little—"

"You don't know how much is too much. No psi, Taemon. Not until your shoulder gets better."

Amma arranged the rocks she had collected to make a circle around the fire. They would place the larger, smoother rocks at the bottom of their bedrolls when it was time to sleep.

Taemon gathered his food and prepared to scoot closer to the fire, but his left arm decided not to cooperate, collapsing under him as he tried to push himself off the ground. His food spilled at his feet. "Oops," he said. "That was clumsy."

Amma pursed her lips. "Here, let me." She gathered up the scattered food and handed it back to Taemon.

"Nature's seasoning," Amma said, pointing to the bits of dirt clinging to his food. "That's what my brothers call it."

Taemon ate a slice of dried apple and nodded. "It adds a woody flavor. With a hint of earthworm. Quite nice, actually."

That at least got a smile out of her, but Taemon could tell that Amma was worried about his injury. Truthfully, he was worried, too. The numbness in his arm did not seem to be improving. There were days when he couldn't feel anything from his fingertips to his shoulder. At least there was no pain involved.

After they'd eaten, Amma set to work on her squirrel snares, whittling sticks and tying pieces of twine to them. Taemon pulled the scarf Challis had given him from his knapsack and ran his hand across the strange design.

"Is that one of Challis's scarves?"

Taemon nodded. "Do you like it?" He wrapped it around his neck and struck a silly pose. "Challis said you would."

"It looks very . . . warm," she said with a laugh.

"Warm is good," Taemon said. "I'm liking warm more and more each day."

Amma got up to check the rocks by the fire. "Then you'll like these rocks. They're just about ready."

A few days back, when the temperature became uncomfortably cold for the first time, Amma had shown Taemon how to heat smooth stones by the fire and use big, glossy leaves they'd gathered to wrap the heated rocks and make bedroll warmers. It was a trick her brothers had taught her.

Taemon thought of his own brother. The only tricks Yens had shown him were the cruel kind, and those were usually aimed at Taemon. He wondered how different his life might have been if he'd grown up with a family like Amma's.

Taemon watched as Amma tied the wrapped rocks with thin vines and placed a couple at the bottom of each of their bedrolls. Later, when he climbed inside his bedroll, the toasty heat warmed his toes. By morning the rocks would be cold, but his bedroll stayed warm long enough for Taemon to fall asleep.

The next morning, Amma had an announcement: "Today's the day we should find the saddle."

"The saddle?"

"That's how it was labeled on the map," Amma said. "It's a dip where two valleys connect, so it probably looks like a saddle. That's where we'll need to cross over."

Taemon frowned. "It can't be that simple. Otherwise people would have crossed the mountain long ago."

"True," Amma said. "But remember that crossing the mountain was forbidden. From what I know of the city, people learn from a young age that they can't do anything without permission. Would any of you even have thought to try to visit the Republik?"

Taemon shook his head. It had certainly never occurred to *him* to try to cross Mount Deliverance, and he'd never heard anyone talk about it, not even Yens, who seemed to think the rules didn't apply to him. Still, he couldn't shake the idea that crossing the mountain was going to be more complicated than hopping over a saddle.

Just getting to the saddle proved difficult. The slope was steep and rocky. Once they had to walk in a crouch for about twenty-five feet in order to pass under a rock roof. Another tough spot required them to remove their packs and slither between the rocks, tugging their packs behind them. Several times they had to scoot on their butts over boulders with little or nothing to hold on to.

"I guess you were right," Amma called up to Taemon as she lowered herself down a crag. "Getting to the saddle isn't simple."

"I would have liked to be wrong," Taemon called back. He walked toward the edge of the crag, turned around, gripped the ledge with both hands, and slowly started to lower himself. Almost immediately his left arm gave out on him. He held on with one hand and found a foothold just before he slipped. He scrambled the rest of the way down and shook out his left arm once he was back on solid ground.

He was glad Amma hadn't seen that. If she knew how much he was struggling, she might insist they turn back.

Next they had to hop across some large rocks strewn in the little valley they were in.

"This isn't so bad," Amma called out as she picked a path from rock to rock.

"I know why you're so far ahead of me," Taemon said, trying to hide how out of breath he was. "It's my scarf, isn't it? You're embarrassed to be seen with me."

Amma laughed. "Who's going to see us? Squirrels?"

Taemon hopped onto the next rock and nearly lost his balance.

"Taemon!"

"I'm okay," he said quickly, jumping to the next rock as if to prove it. "Just lost my balance for a sec —"

"Look!"

He looked up. Amma was pointing at a gap in the rugged mountainside.

"The saddle," she said.

It was the highest point of the path they were on. A narrow canyon led up to it, then there was a slope that was crazy steep and strewn with boulders and loose rocks. That's what they had to get over.

"It looks impossible," Taemon said.

"You mean impassible?"

Taemon nodded. "Same thing."

Amma tilted her head as she peered at the slope. "I wouldn't say impossible. But pretty tough. Let's rest for a bit and enjoy the view."

They sat on an outcropping that looked out over Deliverance.

"Look how far we've come." Amma took a sip from her water bottle.

A jagged ravine lay below them, and far beyond that, the wooded valley of Deliverance. To the south, they could see the cluster of buildings that made up the colony. Directly ahead, to the east, the city of Deliverance was clearly visible, the walls forming a diamond shape around it. Logging camps were visible as well, both the powerless and the abandoned psi-powered ones. Way off in the distance, the hazy line of the ocean wavered in the sunlight.

"It looks so peaceful from here," Taemon said.

Amma murmured her agreement.

Taemon thought about all the turmoil that was going on

right now. The city of former psi wielders trying to adjust to a completely foreign lifestyle without psionic power. The colony struggling to help the city dwellers while also looking after their own people. Deliverance was anything but peaceful at the moment.

After a few more meditative moments, Taemon stood and turned to face the daunting slope they had to cross. Amid the scraggly brush, two squirrels took turns chasing each other.

"Why don't you stay here and get the lunch ready?" Amma suggested. "I'm going to set my snares. If we're lucky, we'll have fresh roasted squirrel tonight."

"Never thought I'd feel lucky to eat a squirrel," Taemon said, fumbling with the zippers on his backpack.

"And I never thought I'd be crossing Mount Deliverance and going to the Republik," Amma responded, grabbing the snares. "Life has a funny way of surprising you."

While Amma was gone, Taemon worked on setting out their lunch. There wasn't much, but it still took a surprisingly long time. He hadn't used psi since rescuing Amma from Free Will's men; why wasn't his arm getting better?

Amma came back right as he finished up. They ate slowly, neither of them in much of a hurry to tackle that monster slope. Taemon took a trip into the bushes to answer the call of nature, and when he got back, Amma was packing up. "We've probably waited long enough," she said. "Let's go see if we'll have meat for dinner."

They stashed their knapsacks among a pile of rocks, more to keep them out of the way of nosy critters than for fear that someone would steal them. Amma carried one of her hunting knives, and as Taemon followed a few steps behind her, he tried not to think about what it would be used for.

Amma led him into the stunted pines and scrubby undergrowth that clung to the mountainside.

"Shh. Stop!" Amma held up her hand.

Taemon looked past her and saw two squirrels standing right next to the snares. If they moved just a few inches to one side, there would be a hearty dinner tonight.

Taemon and Amma waited. The squirrels seemed in no hurry. They darted this way and that, inspecting leaves and searching for some tasty morsel, but never triggering the snares.

Taemon's stomach rumbled. It was hours till dinner-time, but his meager lunch had hardly satisfied him. If they had any hope of making it to the saddle, they would need more than a handful of dried fruit and a few strips of jerky.

He eyed the squirrels closely. All it would take was one little nudge—one little nudge with psi—and they could have not one but *two* fat squirrels for dinner. And one little squinch of psi wasn't going to hurt his shoulder.

But he couldn't push the squirrels. Amma might notice that and get after him. He needed to make it look natural. He looked around for something that would startle the squirrels. All he needed was a pebble or a pinecone, something that might fall on its own.

Nearby was a large boulder with lots of little pebbles scattered around and on top of it. One small rock perched on the edge of the boulder looked like it could drop at any moment. It was perfectly positioned to roll down and herd the squirrels toward the snares. Taemon could make sure it rolled in the right direction. All it would take was the tiniest nudge.

Taemon cleared his mind and gathered his psi. He pictured exactly what he wanted to happen. Then he gave the command. *Be it so!*

The pebble fell and tumbled toward the squirrels. But the squirrels jumped in the opposite direction of the snares. *No! Go the other way!*

Taemon reacted without thinking. He used psi to slide the boulder outward a few inches, which allowed a cascade of pebbles to fall toward the squirrels and force them back to the snares.

The minute he'd done it, he knew it had been a mistake. He felt the weakness in his shoulder spread throughout his body. A roar filled his ears, his own pulse pounding against his eardrums. He felt dizzy, and the whole mountain seemed to vibrate.

"Holy Mother Mountain," Amma whispered. "Is that what I think it is?"

And now Amma knew he'd used psi and had weakened himself. He had been a fool to try such a thing.

"Run!" Amma yelled, yanking Taemon's arm.

Taemon glanced back toward the snares. The small stream of pebbles had become a mighty river of rocks and soil and debris. As they watched, the boulder itself became dislodged and started tumbling down the slope. Rock slide!

They ran, dodging the larger rocks and trying to ignore

the smaller ones that pelted their legs. Worst of all, Taemon could not feel his feet touching the ground. He had to consciously place each foot as he ran. He slipped once, and Amma had to pull him up.

When the rock slide had finally run its course, Taemon and Amma sat down and tried to catch their breath. Their frantic escape had taken them much lower—and farther from the saddle.

"Now, *that*," Amma panted, "was lucky."

"I was thinking more along the lines of *un*lucky," Taemon said. Had she noticed how weak he was?

"Lucky we weren't killed," Amma said between breaths.

"Cha, but look." Taemon pointed to the saddle.

The boulder was now blocking the narrow canyon that led to it. Now the saddle was completely and indisputably impassible. *And* impossible.

And there was no squirrel for dinner.

EIGHT

Hunger is the finest seasoning.

— THE WARRIOR'S SERENITY

For a few silent moments, they stared at the pile of rocks that separated them from the saddle.

"We were so close," Taemon said. "Now how do we cross the mountain?"

"Maybe there's another way," Amma said.

"Somehow I doubt that." One way over the mountain was hard enough to believe. More than one way seemed too much to hope for.

Amma sighed. "Well, then, maybe there's a way around the rock slide. Another way to get to the saddle."

"Maybe," Taemon said. "Or maybe we'll just waste a lot of time looking for something that doesn't exist."

"What do you suggest—that we turn around and go home?"

Taemon couldn't believe that he was now the one doubting this plan and Amma was the one pushing them to keep searching. He couldn't just give up now, not when they'd come this far. So what if his left arm didn't work very well and he limped a little? He knew now not to use psi unless it was a matter of life or death; he could manage to keep going with a bad arm and a limp.

"No, of course not," he said, getting unsteadily to his feet. "Let's keep moving."

They searched among the rocks for their knapsacks and found Taemon's only a few yards away, covered in rocks and dirt. Amma's was nowhere to be found.

"We'll have to make do with what we have," Taemon said, although it was a disheartening prospect: only one bedroll, half the food gone, and some of Drigg's supplies lost as well.

Amma sat down and put her head in her hands. "All our food is gone."

It took him a second to understand what she meant.

"No, it's not," he said. "I saw that you tried to lighten my load. I repacked both packs. My knapsack has half of the food."

But Amma shook her head. "I changed it back right after lunch, when you were off in the bushes. All the food was in my pack. And most of the tools." She took a trembly breath. "I'm sorry."

Taemon knew she shouldn't be the one apologizing. The rock slide had been his fault, but he couldn't bring himself to tell her. It wouldn't fix anything, and it would only make her more worried about his injury. But they'd have to survive the next few days on whatever they could catch.

"I guess we'll have to make sure we get some of those squirrels tonight," Taemon said. The tools were another concern, but he didn't bring it up.

Amma squared her shoulders. "You're right. We can eat squirrels. And there are some edible plants. The snow hasn't killed them off yet."

"Right," Taemon said. "Let's get moving." He hefted his knapsack, which, though it was filled with blankets, felt more like it was filled with rocks. He forced his numb feet to move forward. They had to go down the mountain in order to look for a way around the rock slide. But going *down* meant they would eventually have to go *up* again. He wondered if he could manage it.

Amma was unusually quiet, and Taemon wished he could think of something to lift her spirits.

They came to a stream and a little meadow covered in wildflowers with tiny star-shaped orange blossoms. It was enough to lift anyone's spirits.

"Let's camp here for the night," Taemon said. "Maybe that stream has fish we can catch."

"Good idea," Amma said. "Camping, that is. But there won't be any fish in that stream."

"How do you know?" Taemon asked.

"It's too shallow, and the water's moving too fast." She laughed and jabbed him in the ribs, which he was glad he couldn't feel. "You're such a city boy. Why don't you build a fire and get some water? I'll go set the snares."

She left with the snares and a basket, and Taemon struggled to open his pack. He had no feeling in his fingertips or his feet, and everything on his left side from his shoulder to his foot was numb. He told himself he just needed some time to get over his last psi episode.

After fumbling around inside his knapsack, he discovered that the tinderbox was missing. And the water bottles. And the cook pot. How would they get water? Or build a fire? Even if they caught a squirrel, how would they cook it?

Skies, he was so tired. He couldn't think of what to do. He needed a rest. Just a little rest while Amma was hunting squirrels.

He lay down with his pack as a pillow and fell asleep immediately.

Amma's voice jolted him awake: "No squirrel yet, but I found wild asparagus and some clover."

She stopped when she saw him. "No fire? No water? What happened?"

"Sorry," Taemon said, rubbing his eyes. "There's no tinderbox. I couldn't find the bottles. And I guess I fell asleep."

Amma's shoulders sagged. "I forgot about the tinderbox. Let me see if there's something else we can use." She laid the plants she'd gathered on some clean leaves, then rummaged through the knapsack.

Taemon tried to rub some feeling into his hands. When he stood up, he lost his balance and had to lean against the nearest tree.

"What's wrong?" Amma asked.

"My leg . . ."

"Must have been the rock slide. You could've twisted your ankle when you slipped."

"Maybe I can walk it off." He took a couple steps forward, then stumbled.

"Skies, that's not good." Amma helped him sit down again. "It's the same side as your bad arm, isn't it? It's getting worse."

Taemon shrugged. He'd had the same thought.

"How are you going to walk?"

"I can walk. I just need a sturdy stick, something to support myself on that side. I'll be okay."

"All right. Maybe that'll work."

While Amma built the fire, Taemon unpacked the bedroll and separated the layers to make two thin bedrolls. After that, he sat there feeling useless and guilty. He shouldn't have used psi. The rock slide was his fault. And he'd made himself weaker in the process, which made things harder for Amma.

He took his scarf out and laid it across his lap. He traced a hand over the nubbly yarn. Green, blue, orange, and brown—there was no pattern to speak of, just jagged patches of color. When Challis had given him the scarf, he'd thought the colors were garish. But now he saw how appropriate they were. Brown like the rocks that jutted out from the mountainside. Green like the pine trees. Orange like the tiny wildflowers that covered the meadow. Blue like the stream. The only color in the scarf that wasn't in the landscape around them was a thin, continuous line of silver metallic thread that meandered through each of the other colors.

"Finally!" Amma said as she sat back. She'd gotten a small fire started, Skies only knew how. "We don't have anything to cook, but at least we won't freeze."

Amma divided up the plants, and Taemon started chewing on an asparagus spear. "Not bad."

"Still," Amma said, "roasted squirrel would have been nice."

"I'd rather eat asparagus than squirrel," Taemon said, hoping to lift the gloom.

"Oh?" Amma grinned. "Would you rather eat a maggot or an earthworm?"

Taemon grimaced. "Neither! Don't tell me that's dessert."

Amma laughed. "No. I mean if you had to. If you were starving and had to choose. Maggot or earthworm?"

"Earthworm, definitely," Taemon answered. He thought for a moment. "Would you rather eat a jellyfish or a moth the size of your hand?"

They played would-you-rather until the daylight faded; then they set up the bedrolls under the shelter of some low-lying pine branches. Just before they went to sleep, Taemon said, "Tomorrow will be better. I'll find a stick to help me walk. And we'll find another way to the saddle."

"And we'll catch some squirrels," Amma added.

Taemon laughed. "That's the spirit." He pulled the blanket tight around his shoulders. "Tomorrow everything will be better."

But the next morning, they woke up to find two feet of snow covering the mountain.

NINE

Hope and fear cannot live in the same heart, for one will
drive out the other.

— THE WARRIOR'S SERENITY

The blindingly white world was ghastily beautiful. Low-
hanging clouds shrouded the mountaintop. The air felt
brittle, as if it would shatter with a sharp blow. The whole
mountain seemed hushed with a sacred stillness.

"Skies, I'm freezing," Amma said through chatter-
ing teeth. They already had all their sweaters on, so they
pulled their sleeping blankets around their shoulders.
Taemon tied his scarf around his chin to cover his nearly
frozen ears.

They were able to build a small fire with some dry sticks and dead branches they'd found under the trees, untouched by snow.

"How are we going to do this?" Amma said. "You can barely walk, and this snow is going to make it even harder."

"I just need a walking stick or a crutch," Taemon said. "I can get by with that, snow or no snow."

"Even if we find a stick for you," she said, "I don't know where we're going. The snow makes everything look different. I'm having a hard time getting my bearings. Aren't you?"

Taemon looked up the white mountain slope. Amma was right: even though these were the same views as yesterday, everything looked unfamiliar under two feet of snow.

"I'm not sure it's wise to go on," Amma said.

"Are you saying we should turn back?"

"We have no water. No supplies. No food. Now that the snow is here, the green plants will be frozen. The squirrels will begin their hibernation. If that's not enough, you have a serious injury. We don't know where we're going or even if there's still a way to get there." She turned and looked him in the eye. "We could die out here, Taemon."

"We have to at least try," Taemon said. "Can we just try?"

She held his gaze for a moment, then looked away. Nudging the snow with her foot, she took a deep breath and blew it out. "One try. One. If this doesn't work, we turn back. Deal?"

Taemon nodded. "If it doesn't work, you can turn back."

Amma shook her head. "That's not the deal. The deal is if it doesn't work we *both* turn back. I'm not leaving you out here."

"Okay, okay. Deal," he said. "Let's go."

Amma grabbed his good arm. "Not so fast. Elbow vow."

"What?"

"Come on. Elbow vow. Didn't you do that as a kid?"

"Um, no," Taemon said.

"Here, bend your arm up like this. Good. Now clap your hand with mine . . ."

Taemon tried to follow along as Amma chanted. "Elbow, elbow. Hand. Head. I'll be true until I'm dead."

It was an elaborate ritual that ended with Taemon's palm resting on Amma's forehead, and hers on his.

Amma nodded. "Now it's official."

The first task was to find a walking stick for Taemon.

After several attempts, they finally found something that worked. In a way. It was hard to hold on to the stick without any feeling in his hand. The cold only made it worse.

And the snow. The snow made everything colder, slipperier, trickier. Every step meant wading through snow up to their knees. Not only that, but it was also hard to tell what was under the snow. More than once, Taemon stepped on a concealed rock and lost his balance.

Amma went first and broke a path, but even following in her footsteps was difficult. And the effort of breaking the path was clearly exhausting. They struggled forward for over two hours, sometimes uphill, sometimes descending a bit to find a better path around obstacles. As they came around a group of trees, Amma stopped suddenly. Taemon came up beside her.

"What is—? Oh."

Their campsite. The place where they'd slept under the low branches. The blackened fire circle where they'd stood and made an elbow vow that morning. All that work, and they were back where they started.

"I tried," said Amma. "I really did. But everything looks different covered with snow. I'm not even sure where the saddle is anymore." She shook her head slowly. "Skies, I'm so cold."

"Here," Taemon said, removing his scarf and giving it to Amma.

"Thanks." She wrapped it around her neck and chin. "I hate to say it, but I think it's time to admit defeat."

Her words didn't register. He was staring at the scarf. The orange, the blue, the green, and that thread of silver.

"Do you mind if I . . . ?" He reached out, unwrapped the scarf, and took it from Amma.

"What's wrong?" she asked.

Taemon held up the scarf and traced the blue yarn with his finger. It looked something like a lightning bolt, the way it zigzagged and split. It reminded him of the river they had been following. Yes, the river. And the orange patch would be the meadow. It was situated perfectly, just below the river. In fact . . .

Taemon held the scarf at arm's length. He tilted it one way, then the other, lowered it, then lifted it again.

"What are you doing? Has the cold finally gotten to your brain?" Amma tried to sound teasing, but he could hear genuine concern in her voice.

"We have a map! The scarf. The scarf is a map!"

Amma frowned. "Quit flubbing around. If you're going klonky, then we really do have to go back."

"No, look." Taemon showed her how everything matched perfectly with the landscape. "This silver line is the way we have to go. It will take us over the mountain!"

"Let me see," Amma said, and Taemon held the scarf out for her. He pointed out the rivers and the meadow. "Does it look like the map you remember?"

"No," Amma said. "That map didn't have any colors. It didn't show the meadow or the trees, just the elevation lines. And it showed the path going through the saddle. This silver thread goes much father north." Amma shook her head. "It doesn't make sense. Challis doesn't have her psi anymore. How would she know the way to get over the mountain? And even if she did, why didn't she just tell us the scarf was a map?"

"She made the scarf before the Fall," Taemon said. "But she didn't give it to me until the morning I left. I'm not even sure she knew what it was, or why she needed to give it to me then. But who cares? We know a new way to go now. We can make it!"

Amma let out a sigh. "We had a deal. One try, then we turn back."

"This is different," said Taemon. "Now we have a map."

She glared at him. "We have a scarf. I'm still not convinced it's a map. Besides, can you even follow that thing now that everything's covered in snow?"

Taemon nodded. "We can use this camp as a reference point. We know the meadow was over that way," he said, pointing, "which means we need to go *that* way." He pointed away from the meadow and away from the saddle. "It's a different path, Amma. Maybe it's easier."

"But still, the snow . . . I don't know. . . ."

"One last try," Taemon said. "The very last, I promise. If this doesn't work, we go back. No matter what."

Amma stood there for a moment with her mouth pressed in a thin line. "All right," she finally said. "But this is without a doubt the absolute last try."

"Elbow vow," said Taemon. And this time he did the chanting.

This was it. If this attempt failed, he was certain he wouldn't be able to persuade Amma to try again. Either they made it across the mountain by following the route knitted into the scarf or they went back home. And only the Heart of the Earth could help Da then.

TEN

Weakness is not our darkest fear. More frightening than
weakness is power beyond measure.

— THE WARRIOR'S SERENITY

"I don't know about this," Amma said. "Shouldn't we be
going *toward* the Republik instead of away from it?"

Taemon shrugged. He tried to steady his stride, plant-
ing the walking stick firmly each time. It made him feel
determined. Resolved. He was going to get over the mountain. He had to. "Maybe heading away from it will lead us
to a place where we can go toward it."

Amma grunted. "I'm not sure that makes sense, but
we'll see."

Taemon calmed his mind and let the lopsided rhythm of his stride lull his thoughts.

They walked and walked, this time with Taemon in front, navigating with the scarf, and Amma following. After an hour or so, Taemon's confidence began to wane. According to the scarf map, they were nearing the end of the silver line, yet they were clearly nowhere near the top of the mountain. They were in a long, narrow valley with a thousand little nooks and crannies. Taemon stopped to look around and compare his surroundings with the scarf. Amma looked over his shoulder.

"I think the scarf is telling us to go this way." Amma pointed to a pile of boulders that looked vaguely like a nappy brown spot on the scarf. "But it's a dead end."

Taemon longed to use clairvoyance to check for some kind of hidden passage, but he knew what would happen if he did. He would weaken himself to the point of not being able to walk at all. That would be no help.

"Let's see," Taemon said, holding the scarf this way, then that.

"Look, the silver line goes here, and then it just ends," Amma said, pointing over his shoulder. "That can't be right. I hate to say this, Taemon, but sometimes a scarf is just a scarf."

Taemon looked at the rocks, then at the scarf, then at the rocks again. He hobbled over to a boulder and tried to climb on top, but his legs weren't strong enough. He looked back at Amma. "Could you give me a boost?"

She frowned, but she walked over and laced her hands together to boost him up. He scrabbled awkwardly over the boulder, then jumped down—though it was more of a fall than a jump—on the other side, taking care to bear most of his weight on his right leg. He looked around. Rocks, rocks, and more rocks. His heart dropped.

But just as he was about to climb back over the boulder, he noticed an odd shadow between two other boulders. Was that a . . . ?

"Amma! Come quick! I think I found something."

She clambered over the boulder and slid next to him.

"It's a cave," she said, sounding unimpressed.

"Maybe," Taemon agreed, but his gut was telling him it was more than that. When he stepped inside, the darkness made it hard to see much of anything. He stumbled over a large rock and had to catch himself.

"That must have hurt," Amma said.

"Not that much," he answered. "I can't feel very much in that foot." As he pushed himself to his feet, he realized that it was not a rock that had tripped him, but a metal box.

"Take a look at this." Taemon pushed the box toward the door of the cave, where there was more light. He tried the latch and found it wasn't locked.

"Wait," Amma said. "That might not be a good idea. We have no idea what that is or who put it there."

Taemon turned to face her. "This could tell us about the people who've traveled this way before."

"All right," Amma agreed, stepping closer. "But be careful."

Taemon lifted the lid.

"Supplies," she said. "Food, bottles of water, some blankets."

Taemon grabbed the blanket, shook it, and spread it out in the weak sunlight. "Psi woven. This blanket is from Deliverance."

Amma nodded. "Those bottles look like they're from the city, too."

"I don't understand," Taemon said. "I thought my da was

kidnapped by the Republik. Why would he have brought supplies with him—supplies enough for a dozen men?"

"Maybe the kidnappers stole supplies in Deliverance and brought them along on the return trip," Amma said.

"And left them here?" Taemon said.

"You're right. That doesn't make sense. All we can say is that someone from Deliverance has come this way."

"And that's a good sign, right?" Taemon looked Amma in the eye. "That means we're on the right path and we should keep going."

Amma was quiet for a while, studying the supplies. "Maybe this box was Elder Naseph's doing. If he was negotiating an alliance with the Republik, maybe he was smuggling supplies across the mountain."

Amma began packing some of the food and water into their knapsack.

Taemon's conscience was tugging at him. "Isn't that stealing?"

Amma stood and looked him in the eye. "We don't have a choice, Taemon. If you want to keep going, we'll have to take these supplies."

Together they packed a few more things into the knapsack.

"Let's not take all of it," Taemon said. "In case someone does need this stuff."

Amma nodded. "We can't fit it all, anyway."

At the bottom of the box, Taemon found a flashlight, and before Amma could argue, he used the tiniest bit of psi to turn it on. He felt the now-familiar weakening but tried to ignore it.

"Hey," Amma protested. "No psi, remember?"

"How else are we going to get through the tunnel?"

"Tunnel?" Amma asked. "Is that what this is?"

"Let's find out."

The first part was a shallow cave that looked completely natural. But when Taemon stepped a bit farther in and cast the flashlight across the back wall, he noticed an opening just wide enough for one person to walk through without ducking.

"It *is* a tunnel!" he said.

Amma looked dubious. "It could just be the way the rocks settled. I don't want you to get your hopes up."

Taemon walked forward a few more feet. "It just keeps going!" He stopped and shone the light on the wall of the tunnel. He ran his hand over the rock. It was smooth, with no marks that might indicate a chisel or a shovel or any other kind of powerless digging.

"It was made with psi, wasn't it?" Amma said, coming up beside him.

"It had to be." He marveled at the thought. Only an incredibly powerful psi wielder could tunnel through solid rock. Had Nathan made it all those years ago when he first pulled up the mountains that protected Deliverance? Or had someone—or a team of someones—made it in recent years? "It's hard to tell how long it's been here," he said.

Amma gave a low whistle. "Skies, this might work after all."

They moved forward, Taemon first with the flashlight and Amma behind him. "I'm just glad we don't have to tromp through any more snow," she said. "Tunnels I can handle."

Taemon wasn't sure how long they'd been in the tunnel. An hour? Two hours? Luckily it sloped downward, making it a bit easier on his left leg. The air had a stale smell. Taemon ran a finger along the wall and felt a thin film of moisture clinging to it. He expected to see spiders or insects of some kind, but so far the tunnel seemed devoid of life.

"Are you sure this is going to work?" Amma asked. "The way we're twisting and turning, we could end up back on the Deliverance side."

It was true. The tunnel twisted and curved, and he wondered why. If he were to make a tunnel through a mountain using psi, he would make it straight. This winding path was taking forever.

"This has to be it." The secret path to the Republik. What would it be like? It was exciting and terrifying at the same time.

The flashlight chose that moment to die, blanketing them in utter darkness. They stumbled to a stop.

"Great," Amma whispered.

"I'm surprised it didn't happen sooner," Taemon said. "This kind needs sunlight to recharge."

He heard her sigh. "Well, there's not much we can do about it. We'll just have to feel along the walls."

Taemon had one hand on his walking stick and one hand on the wall. Behind him, Amma placed her hand on his shoulder. It felt good, like they were connected. It also felt heavy, like a responsibility pressing down on him.

After at least another hour trudging through the dark tunnel, Amma squeezed his shoulder. "I think . . . I think the blackness is turning gray."

Taemon blinked. "You're right. We must be close to the end!"

"Skies, don't say it like that," Amma whispered.

They picked up their pace as the visibility improved. The tunnel widened, and they had to climb over a few more rocks, which meant Taemon once again needed Amma's help. Finally, they came to a rocky outcropping at the mouth of the tunnel.

Taemon was ready to step out of the tunnel, but Amma held back.

"I need a minute for my eyes to adjust," she said, shielding her face with one arm. "I can't even see where I'm going."

The light was nearly as blinding as the darkness had been. But after a few minutes of blinking and rubbing his eyes, Taemon realized that the light wasn't that bright; it was just that the sun was low in the sky and glaring right at them. It would be twilight soon. They had been inside the tunnel all afternoon.

He turned to look at Amma, who was staring out over the land. She turned to him and gave him a quick hug. "We made it!"

"We did," whispered Taemon. "We're in the Republik."

"No snow." Amma beamed. "It's warmer here."

Taemon looked again and saw that Amma was right. On this side, they were below the snow line, and it was definitely warmer. Taemon took his jacket off and tied it around his waist. The warmth on his skin felt heavenly.

Everything was different on this side of the mountain— the sparseness of the trees, the vegetation, the color of the soil. The differences were subtle, but this was definitely not Deliverance.

There were no paths this high on the mountain, and the trees were few and far between. Looking down, they could see signs of houses and buildings among the heavily forested hills. The buildings were spread out, not clustered together as a city would be. Some of them looked rather large, though it was hard to tell from this far away.

"What do you think those buildings are for?" Taemon asked.

Amma shook her head slowly. "I have no idea. I guess

we'll find out tomorrow. Right now we need to find a place to camp before it gets dark."

"Wait. Look over there." Taemon pointed to some movement far below them.

Someone was running up the slope of the mountain. A woman, from the look of her long black hair and the dress she was wearing.

"Skies, is that a jaguar chasing her?" Amma said.

Taemon looked beyond the woman and saw the blur of a very large cat. "That looks bad."

It was hard to judge the woman's speed, but she must have been fast because the jaguar was not gaining. Or maybe the jaguar was trying to tire her out before going in for the kill.

"I can't watch," Amma said.

Taemon felt the same, yet he couldn't seem to look away. "Just a minute. I see more people." A group of uniformed men was chasing after the jaguar. "The authorities are going to help her."

Both Taemon and Amma startled when the sound of guns echoed against the mountain.

"They're shooting at the jaguar," Taemon said.

Amma shuddered. "I don't want to see the jaguar killed either."

"Don't worry—they've missed. Everyone's still running," Taemon said.

As soon as he said that, the woman slowed down and turned to face the jaguar.

"Skies, does she think she can fight a jaguar?" Amma said. It seemed she couldn't look away either.

But the jaguar didn't attack the woman. Instead, it ran up to her and stood by her side. Together, the woman and the cat faced the men who chased them.

"What in the Great Green Earth . . . ?" Amma breathed.

More gunshots rang out, but the jaguar and the woman seemed unhurt.

She was gathering psi. Taemon couldn't say how he knew that. It was almost as if he could feel it. Before he could tell Amma what was happening, though, three of the soldiers fell to the ground. The woman was wielding an incredible amount of psi, so much that the air fairly rang with it.

Taemon tried to follow what she was doing, but it was all happening so fast. Guns flew from soldiers' hands and disassembled as they arced backward, the parts falling inertly to the ground. The disarmed men were at a loss for what to do. Then one by one they dropped, clutching their throats or heads or chests. One man was lying with a pool of blood under his head.

"Holy . . ." Amma muttered.

Psi. The woman had used psi to kill those men. How in the Burning Blazes was that possible? Was she from Deliverance? Even if she was, she would be powerless. She was clearly defending herself, which explained why she was able to use psi to harm another person, but the fact that she used psi at all was unthinkable. Only Nathan's people had the gift of psi. That is, they used to.

The woman turned and continued running up the slope with the jaguar at her heels. She was heading directly toward them.

ELEVEN

Only the pain of a new experience can break the shell that limits understanding.

— THE WARRIOR'S SERENITY

Amma tugged Taemon's arm. "Quick. Back in the tunnel."

"No," Taemon said. "If that woman follows us, I don't want to fight her in a tunnel."

He jumped down from the ledge they'd been standing on, and Amma did the same. There were few places to hide. There were no trees close by, but there were plenty of rocks. Unfortunately, none of them was big enough to hide behind. The best they could do was squeeze into a little niche under the ledge. It should be out of sight from the direction in which the woman was approaching.

They'd lost sight of the woman when they'd jumped down, but Taemon could hear her footsteps. The jaguar's, too.

Then the footsteps stopped.

A menacing growl made Taemon's blood run cold.

"I know you're there," said a voice. "I saw you earlier. You can come out. My battle is not with you." The voice was raspy, out of breath, but Taemon could still hear the strange accent. She was definitely not from Deliverance.

Taemon looked steadily at Amma. "There's no hiding from that jaguar," he whispered.

"She wants to talk," Amma whispered back. "Maybe she's not so bad."

The jaguar let out an ear-piercing scream, which made it clear that the time for hiding was over.

Taemon gathered psi at the ready, just in case he had to defend himself, and stepped forward to face the woman.

Only it wasn't a woman. It was a boy. A teenager. His long hair fell nearly to his waist. He wore black leather leggings and a matching sleeveless tunic fastened with heavy metal clasps.

The boy squinted at Taemon. "Who are you?"

"How did you do that just now?" Taemon asked,

nodding toward where the boy had come from, where he'd destroyed the men chasing him. It was a foolish question. He knew exactly how it had been done. With psi. But how did this boy have psi? It didn't make sense!

Taemon felt Amma's hand on his arm, but he didn't dare take his eyes off the boy, who had just used psi to kill seven people.

As he and the boy stood there, facing off, Taemon sensed movement to his left. Skies! He'd forgotten about the jaguar. It pounced on him.

In a split-second reaction, Taemon reached out with psi to stop the fierce cat. The animal jerked back, as if someone had yanked it on a leash, and Taemon heard it cry out with an eerie yelp.

"Don't hurt her!" shouted the boy.

Taemon withdrew his psi—which was a mistake, because the jaguar immediately turned to attack him. In a flash of teeth and fur, hot breath and glowing eyes, the huge cat was on him. What was worse, the cat was pressing down its massive paws on his bad shoulder, which sent a stabbing pain radiating down his spine. The pain made it difficult to focus enough to use psi effectively. If Taemon couldn't keep the cat's sharp claws and wicked teeth from tearing into him, he knew he would lose this battle in a few short moments.

He heard Amma's voice pleading, yelling, but he couldn't focus enough to make out the words. In the instant Taemon was certain he would die, the boy shouted at the jaguar.

"Jix, let him go!"

The beast held Taemon in place for a few extra seconds and growled as if to remind everyone who the victor was. When the jaguar released him, Taemon let out a deep breath. The cat trotted to the boy, who cooed a few words of praise, and settled itself at his feet.

Taemon, meanwhile, was fighting to keep from blacking out. He lay on his back, trying to slow his breathing and focus his vision. He was glad they were done hiking for the day, because he didn't think he could so much as walk right now.

Amma was at his side. "Are you okay?"

"Cha," Taemon said, though he wasn't sure.

"Is that your pet?" Amma asked the boy.

"Jix is not a pet," he said. "More like a traveling companion."

"Still. It's tame?"

"*Tame* isn't the right word, either. We have an understanding."

Taemon sat up slowly, and a tense moment passed as the two boys eyed each other. The Republikite boy's sleeveless tunic showed off the muscles in his arms and shoulders; he was a couple of years older than Taemon.

"So," Taemon said, rising unsteadily to his feet, "what now?"

Amma glanced at the horizon, where the sun was just about to disappear. "I say we make camp and then get to know one another."

Amma, Taemon, and the boy sat in a triangle, cautiously eyeing one another. Jix, the jaguar, lay nearby. The sun was now below the horizon, so the boy pulled out what appeared to be a small lantern and placed it in the center. The strange thing was that the boy used his hand to turn it on, just like a powerless person. But he was obviously not powerless.

Then again, everything about him was strange. His clothes were heavy, nothing like the light psi fabric from the city but somehow more sophisticated than the rustic clothing from the colony. And his hair . . . What kind of boy wore hair that long? He even had an odd smell, but maybe that was the jaguar.

"I'm Amma, born under the Water sign. And this is Taemon. He's a Knife."

The boy frowned and jerked his chin to the side, flipping his hair over his shoulder. "I'm Gevri."

Taemon and Amma waited for him to tell his birth sign, which would shed much more light on his disposition than just his name. But he was not polite enough to include that information.

"You have dominion, don't you?" Gevri asked. "Which means you're from the other side of the mountain. What are you doing here?" He sounded more than curious. He sounded . . . *excited.*

"Dominion?" Taemon asked. "Is that what you call it? You used it to kill those men just now, didn't you?"

"I didn't kill them," Gevri snapped. He shot a fiery glare at Taemon.

"We saw you," Taemon said. "We watched the whole thing."

"They're not dead. I disabled them."

Taemon and Amma exchanged a glance. There was no way to know if this Gevri was telling the truth. It sure looked like he'd killed them. But if they were still alive, then what exactly did "disabled" mean?

"So, is it true? Does everyone in your city have dominion?" Gevri's tone held no trace of anger now. He was back to sounding excited.

Taemon hesitated. How much could he tell this stranger?

"I thought people in the Republik didn't have those powers," Amma said.

"Yeah, well, they don't," Gevri said. "For the most part."

That "yeah" sounded so strange coming from a kid. *Yeah* was a word that Taemon's great-grandparents might have used.

"For the most part?" Taemon repeated. "What does that mean?"

Gevri's eyes narrowed. "What are you two doing here, anyway? You shouldn't be here."

"We're looking for someone," Taemon said. "My father's missing, and we have reason to believe he came to the Republik."

Gevri seemed to consider this. "I know of one person who came here from Nathan's City. Perhaps he is your father."

"I knew it," Taemon said, his pulse quickening. "Do you know where he is? Is he okay?"

Gevri frowned. He reached for a twig and twirled it with his fingers over and over.

A sour worry tightened in Taemon's stomach. Something was going on here, something Gevri didn't want to talk about.

"My guess is that you shouldn't be here, either," Amma said softly after a while, looking at Gevri.

Gevri's expression hardened. "I'm leaving Kanjai. For good. My father, he . . ." He turned to the jaguar and massaged the huge cat's back. "I'm not going back. Ever."

"Okay," Amma said. "So you ran away from home. But what made you want to go over the mountain?"

Gevri didn't answer right away. A barely audible rumble came from the direction of the cat, which Taemon took to be the jaguar version of a purr.

"I'm an archon," Gevri said. "But you've already figured that out."

"A what?" Taemon and Amma asked at the same time.

Gevri looked at them quizzically. "An archon. I have dominion. Why are you so surprised? In your city, everyone's an archon." He stiffened. "Who are you? Did my father send you?"

Gevri jumped to his feet, tossing his head and flipping his hair behind his shoulder. He held his chin high. "You tell my father I'm dead. I am dead to him, and he to me. I am not a soldier anymore, and that's final. As final as death."

The jaguar was on its feet, too, although Taemon couldn't remember seeing it move. It stood poised and taut, ready to attack.

Skies, this boy's moods changed in the blink of an eye!

"Relax," Amma said. "We've got nothing to do with your father."

"We have that in common, at least." Gevri's shoulders relaxed, and he sat down again. "If you're truly from Nathan's City, tell me, what is it like? Is it beautiful? A whole city of archons able to use their powers for good. It must be so peaceful."

Amma and Taemon exchanged a look, an unspoken question passing between them: How much do we tell him?

Taemon cleared his throat. "It can be. But people there are like people anywhere. We have our disagreements and our differences." That was putting it mildly. "Tell us about your city."

"Kanjai? That's not a city. It's the name of the province. Those buildings you see down there are the Kanjai Military Outpost. Way over here next to Nathan's Mountain—that's about as far out as an outpost can get. Which suits my father's purpose."

Military outpost? Taemon did not like the sound of that. And what was Gevri's father's purpose? Gevri's tone had been rather dark, which didn't bode well.

Amma asked the next question: "So, what do people do in a military outpost?"

Gevri shrugged. "Train soldiers, mostly. Some manufacturing since the mines are so close. There's a big medical facility."

Skies, all of this had been happening just on the other side of Mount Deliverance?

The shock must have shown on their faces, because Gevri started laughing. "Gods, you don't know about the war, do you?"

"Just that there is one," Taemon said carefully. "We're not even sure who you're fighting."

Gevri laughed. "Now I know for sure you're from the

other side of the mountain." He grabbed a twig and started drawing shapes in the dirt near the lantern.

"The enemy is the Nau, nine nations that joined together against the Free World." He glanced up and saw their blank expressions. "The Free World are the countries that refuse to give up their sovereign status to the Nau and its regime, its endless regulations and committees. There are only a few of us left now. That's the Republik, here"— he made a mark in the dirt—"and four countries on two other continents, here and here.

"But, see, on either side of the Republik are Nau nations—here and here." He made marks in the dirt to the north and south of the Republik. "We're smack in the middle. We either keep fighting or we lose our country and our freedom."

The pieces were starting to fall into place for Taemon. If Gevri's rough map was to be believed, then Deliverance bordered the easternmost edge of the Republik, which meant that the city of Deliverance was situated next to a prime location for a seaport. It also meant that if either of the Nau nations seized the city, they could invade the Republik as a united force.

Deliverance would be a valuable prize to any of these nations.

"The war has been going on for decades," Gevri continued, "but mostly on the other side of the continent, in the West. Lately, things are heating up here in the East, and my father says that if we don't throw something new at them, something they've never seen before, we could be in trouble. He thinks the archons could save this country."

Taemon tried to catch Amma's eye in the lantern light, to see if she'd noticed the same things that he had. But it was too dark to see much of anything except the diagram in the dirt. When he spoke to Gevri, he tried to make his voice sound casual. "I'm curious about these archons. How exactly does your father plan to use them?"

Gevri frowned, and Taemon could see he was torn. He might not believe in what his father was doing, but that didn't necessarily mean he was ready to compromise his father's plans by sharing them with two complete strangers. "Let's just say that it involves training archons to hone their skills for military purposes. I think that's why they brought your father here, to help with the training. Who better than one of Nathan's men to show us how to master dominion?"

Taemon swallowed. And what would they do with Da when they realized he was powerless?

"So let me get this straight," Amma said. "Everyone in the Republik has . . . dominion, but your dad is training some of them to use their power as a weapon?"

Gevri shook his head. He looked around as though he needed to be sure they were truly alone before he explained. "Not everyone. Only the archons have dominion. And no one knows about the archons except the people at the outpost. Not even the rest of the army knows about them. It's classified."

Wonderful. A supersecret army of archons that the Republikite army didn't even know about. And Da was supposed to be training them!

"So why are you telling us?" Taemon asked warily.

Gevri shrugged. "You've seen what I can do. There's no point denying it. Besides, if you're here to rescue your dad," he said, nodding at Taemon, "then I'm pretty sure that means you and I are on the same side."

Taemon wasn't so sure about that.

Gevri yawned. "Look, we can finish getting to know

one another in the morning. Jix and I are beat. Aren't we, girl? We'll set up camp nearby and see you in the morning." The jaguar gave an impressive yawn, her enormous teeth glinting in the lantern light.

"One last question," Taemon said as Gevri gathered up his things.

"Yeah?"

"These archons . . . They have powers? Still, I mean? They haven't had any, you know, loss of . . . archon-ness?"

Gevri hesitated, then laughed. "Of course not! You're testing me, aren't you? You either have dominion or you don't. Gods!"

"He can be very testy," Amma said, making a joke out of it. "Good night, Gevri."

"Cha, good night," Taemon muttered distractedly.

How? How did these people have psi? Even if it was true that psi existed outside of Deliverance—and despite what Gevri might say, and what they'd seen him do, that was still a pretty big *if*—Taemon had gotten rid of psi, hadn't he? So why would the archons still have "dominion"?

Let me help you remember.

Oh, Skies. The Heart of the Earth was talking to him again.

He saw himself in the past, at the temple, when everything was going wrong and Yens was destroying the temple with an earthquake. He remembered what the Heart of the Earth had said to him then.

You must choose. On behalf of your people, you must choose.

He remembered the turmoil he had felt, trying to decide if taking away psi from the world was the right thing to do. Once again, he heard the words in his mind, the words he'd said to the Heart of the Earth:

Let all psi in Deliverance be done away. Let each man and woman work by the power of his own hands. Let this begin the Great Cycle.

Great Earth and Skies! He had taken away psi from his people, the men and women in Deliverance. He hadn't taken it from the whole world. But then, he'd never imagined that psi existed anywhere else.

When Taemon's breath returned, it was shaky and shallow. The city of Deliverance was now the most vulnerable place on the planet.

TWELVE

That which we despise in others leads to understanding ourselves.

— THE WARRIOR'S SERENITY

The next morning, the call of nature woke Taemon. Amma was still asleep, and there was no sign of Gevri yet. Taemon wondered if the boy would run back to tattle to his father about the two strangers he'd just met from over the mountain. Skies, he hoped not.

Taemon stretched and stood slowly, still sore from his run-in with the jaguar the night before. He shook his left arm, trying to get rid of the numbness, and took a few steps away from the campsite.

A low, rumbling growl made him freeze in his tracks. He felt it more than he heard it.

Taemon looked up to see Gevri's jaguar on a rock just above him. Head low, shoulders high, ears pressed back, it stared at him.

In the symbolism of day signs, the Jaguar stood for aggression or attack, and Taemon was feeling that keenly from the menacing cat. They locked eyes for a moment, then suddenly the jaguar was inside his head, invading his thoughts.

Startled, Taemon took a step back. The animal was not sending coherent thoughts, as the Heart of the Earth did, but rather impressions. Strong impressions: a fierce sense of loyalty to Gevri, a sense that the jaguar would do anything to protect the boy. The cat seemed to be searching Taemon for signs of anything that threatened Gevri even in the slightest.

Taemon's first instinct was to turn and run, but he thought better of it. If the cat wanted assurance that Taemon was no threat, running away would send the wrong signal. He forced himself to hold his ground and calm his thoughts.

Unsure if it would work, he reached out to the jaguar with his thoughts. *I wish no harm. No harm to Gevri. No harm to you. No harm.*

An impression of tenuous satisfaction flitted through Taemon's head, then the cat withdrew. The beast rose to its full height, turned, and sauntered away.

Taemon exhaled. Skies, that was the eeriest thing ever, having a cat connect with his mind like that. He missed the good old days when he had his brain to himself.

When Taemon returned to the campsite, Amma was awake and Gevri was with her. Amma was pulling out some of the food they'd found in the tunnel.

"I'm so glad to see you using your hands for things like this," Gevri said. "I wondered if people in Nathan's City used dominion for everyday stuff like eating, drinking, and brushing hair. That's obviously not true."

Amma froze for a moment, her eyes locked with Taemon's. Gevri thought she had psi. And why wouldn't he? They hadn't told him about the Fall, nor had they explained about the powerless colony. In all the excitement and confusion last night, they hadn't even thought about Gevri expecting to see them using psi!

"So, you don't like using dominion to eat?" Amma said cautiously. Her movements were slow and self-conscious as she laid out the food.

"It's just so weird," Gevri said.

"What's so weird about it?" Taemon asked, moving to help Amma with the food. Her shoulders relaxed a bit when he was beside her, which made him feel good.

"We're trained to use dominion for warfare, and nothing else," Gevri explained. "It's too sacred for mundane tasks. Using dominion for things like eating, drinking, or ordinary everyday lifting is considered profane."

"Wait," Taemon said. "It's not okay to use your sacred power to eat, but it's okay to use it for war? How is hurting people sacred?"

Gevri seemed taken aback. "In the Republik, there's nothing more sacred than war. It's defending your home, your family, your gods. Nothing is more sacred than that."

"That's so . . . different," Amma said slowly. *Different* was an understatement!

Gevri reached into his bag and produced some round, grainy baked disks. "It's what we know. War has become our culture, our industry, our education. Everything centers on war."

"So why are you leaving?" Taemon asked. "There is no war in Deliverance—I mean, Nathan's City." *At least, not yet.*

"The army has taken things too far. They're not just defending anymore. My father especially. He . . . Well, let's just say I feel I have more in common with the peaceful people of Nathan's City than I do with my father."

"Let's eat," Taemon said. "With or without dominion."

Amma handed out the food. Gevri offered them some of his baked disks.

"These are delicious!" Amma said, smiling with her mouth full. "What are they?"

"They're called samkins," Gevri said. "My mother used to make them."

Taemon could sense that there was more to that comment, but before he could ask, the jaguar strolled into the campsite and sat down next to Gevri.

Taemon edged away. "You should have told me your jaguar was an archon."

Amma swallowed the last of her samkin. "That's ridiculous. How can an animal have psi?"

"I don't know," Taemon said. "But that cat can do some really bizarre things."

"You still call it psi?" Gevri said.

"Yes," Taemon said, wondering at the word *still*. "But none of our animals has it. Of course, we're not a nation of warmongers."

Gevri gave Taemon a cold glare. "You shouldn't speak of things you know nothing about."

Amma looked at the jaguar. "I think she's beautiful."

"You can pet her if you like," Gevri said. "She doesn't mind."

Taemon huffed. "I'd rather pet a shark."

But Amma walked over and scratched the cat between its ears. "We're all friends now, aren't we?"

Not exactly, thought Taemon, eyeing both the cat and its master.

After breakfast, Gevri went off with Jix to "have a look around." He wanted to be sure his father hadn't sent soldiers after him.

"I don't trust him," Taemon said as soon as Gevri was out of sight.

"Why not?" asked Amma, sounding genuinely perplexed.

"Don't you think it's a little *convenient* that a disgruntled solider should happen to decide to run away to Deliverance the very day you and I arrive in the Republik?"

Amma frowned. "But no one knew we were coming. What else could it be *but* a coincidence?"

But Taemon had thought about this. "How do we know these archons only have the one form of psi?" he asked, whispering now even though Gevri was long gone. "What if one of them is like Challis and saw us coming?"

"No," Amma said doubtfully. "Gevri would have mentioned such a power."

"Not if he's working for them! Think about it: How did Gevri know about the tunnel? And what has he really told us about my da? This could all be some sort of trap, to lure us into a false sense of security."

Amma started packing away her bedroll. "Okay," she said slowly. "Let's just pretend for a minute that you're right. So what's the trap? He's heading to the city, and we're heading to the military outpost. We would have done that even if we'd never met him."

"Just because we can't see his plan doesn't mean he doesn't have one," Taemon argued, but even he had to admit that he was sounding a bit paranoid now. "I'd just feel a whole lot better if we didn't let Gevri out of our sight."

"Looks like you're about to get your wish," Amma said, nodding toward the top of a hill. "Here he comes now."

They watched as Gevri and Jix raced down the hill, looking for all the world like a kid playing with his pet.

"Beautiful morning!" Amma called brightly.

"Yeah." Gevri pulled a flask from his waistband and took a generous gulp of water. "It looks like it's going to be a beautiful day. Perfect for travel."

Taemon and Amma exchanged a look.

"Why don't you come with us?" Amma blurted out.

"What?"

"Come with us to the outpost. We could really use your help sneaking in."

Gevri shook his head. "You saw the soldiers my father sent. If I go back, they'll kill me. Or try to force me to be a soldier. And I won't be a soldier."

"Your father sent those soldiers?" Amma asked.

"To him, I'm a traitor." Gevri's mouth tightened. "I don't know how things are on your side of the mountain, but in the Republik, there's nothing worse than a traitor."

Taemon thought about the iron rule of Elder Naseph before the Fall, about being banished to the powerless colony. Perhaps Deliverance and the Republik were more alike than anyone realized.

"That's okay," Taemon said, trying to sound a little too relieved. "We can go on our own. We can just ask around until we find the archon trainees. We'll be fine."

Gevri rolled his eyes. "You can't just walk into a military outpost and ask around. They'll arrest you. Besides, even if you *do* manage to sneak into the outpost, you'll never find the archons on your own. They're the best-kept secret in the Republik. If your da really is with them, you have no chance of finding him."

"All the more reason why we need you," Amma said.

Gevri opened his mouth to argue, but Amma cut him off. "If you'll help us find Taemon's father, we'll help you get to Deliverance."

"I know where Nathan's City is," said Gevri. "Just on the other side of this mountain."

Amma raised one eyebrow. Taemon was glad not to be on the receiving end of that look. "Knowing which side of the mountain it's on is hardly the same thing as knowing how to get there. It's much more rugged on our side of the mountain. There are lots of dead-end canyons and dangerous drop-offs. We almost had to turn back more than once."

"And there's snow," Taemon added. "It's colder on the Deliverance side than it is here."

Gevri rubbed his hand across his jaw, deliberating. "So if I help you find your father, you'll escort me to Nathan's City — to Deliverance?"

Taemon hesitated. Would he and Amma really be willing to make good on their promise, to expose the vulnerability of Deliverance to their sworn enemy? Even if that enemy helped them find Taemon's da?

Taemon took a deep breath and then nodded. "Once we find my da, we'll take you with us back to Deliverance."

THIRTEEN

Old friends are best. But remember that old friends are
made from new friends.

— THE WARRIOR'S SERENITY

It wasn't that far from the tunnel to the edge of the outpost. It wouldn't have taken them two days to get there
if they'd gone directly, but Gevri thought it best to wend
their way through the wilderness in order to avoid run-ins
with soldiers. Taemon couldn't argue with that.

The jaguar traveled with them, sometimes disappearing
into the brush, sometimes padding along next to Gevri.

"Where does she go?" Amma asked.

Gevri shrugged. "She checks everything out, on the
lookout for anything dangerous. Sometimes she hunts."

The cat still made Taemon uneasy, but he knew better than to bring that up again. Instead, he felt it was high time he asked the most burning question: "How exactly are there archons in the Republik? I thought the Republikites feared psi—or dominion, as you call it. That's why Nathan put up the mountain."

"Most people *are* afraid of dominion. They don't like the idea of people doing things with their minds. They think it's evil, or spooky at the very least, and want nothing to do with it.

"But my father is different. He thinks dominion will be the ultimate military weapon. Father studied everything he could about psi, which he called *dominion* because he wanted to differentiate it from Nathan's powers. He'd studied weapon science at university and combined all of that knowledge into an experimental program: me."

"You were an experiment?" Amma asked.

Gevri turned to the jaguar. "Jix and I both. I also happened to be his son, an infant at the time. He raised me to believe that I had these powers. Apparently, that's all it takes."

"There's more to it than that," Taemon said defensively. "Children have the unique ability to acquire psi, but they must be raised knowing that psi is possible. If your father was able to convince you of this without any examples to show you, he must be an incredible teacher."

Gevri nodded. "I was isolated from other children until I was thirteen years old. My father didn't want me to realize that other kids didn't have dominion. He feared it might make me give up on my own powers. Father doesn't have psi himself, but when I was very young, he made it look like he did, so that I would grow up thinking certain things were possible. He's become an expert on such things."

"What about Jix?" Amma asked. "Does your father know that she has dominion?"

Gevri hesitated. "Yes, though I doubt he understands the extent of it. Jix and I . . . well, let's just say we look out for each other."

There was a sadness in Gevri's voice just then that made Taemon think there was more to that story. Taemon eyed the cat warily. "So she's the only animal in the Republik with dominion?"

Gevri nodded. "For a while he was experimenting with breeding animals to increase their capacity for dominion. It worked, to some extent, but he could never control the animals, so he had them killed. I tried to save them, but Jix was the only one that I could—" Gevri's voice broke, and he cleared his throat. "Jix is the only one."

As sad as that was, Taemon was glad he wouldn't be encountering more animals with psi. "But you're not the only archon. You said there were others."

"I was the first. My father succeeding in bringing out dominion in me, but he failed in other respects. Despite his best efforts, my personality traits weren't right. I was not aggressive enough."

"Not aggressive?" Taemon interrupted. "I saw you handle those soldiers. That seemed plenty aggressive."

"No, that was defensive," Gevri said shortly. "There is a big difference between the two."

"So what happened when your father determined that you weren't cut out to be an archon?" Amma asked.

"He couldn't very well just let me go," Gevri explained. "I'd spent my whole life in the military outpost, save for a few missions in the Republik. What if someone started asking too many questions? Or what if I accidentally used dominion?" It was clear by the way Gevri said these words that they were not his but his father's. The father's contempt for his son was all too clear. "So my father gave me a choice: toughen up and become an archon solider or spend the rest of my life locked behind bars. I chose a third option."

Taemon and Amma followed along behind Gevri without speaking, each too lost in thought. What kind of father would threaten to imprison his son for life? What kind of son would betray his own father?

They were quiet for some time. Then Gevri suddenly continued talking.

"A few months ago, Father got his hands on some old books about psi. I snuck into his office and read them."

Taemon heard Amma gasp. He looked at Gevri to see if he'd noticed her response, but if he had, he didn't let on. He kept talking.

"That's when I understood that psi wasn't supposed to be a weapon. It was supposed to be peaceful, to enable people to do good things for one another. My whole life, my whole family, everything has been centered on war. The idea of a society built around peace was fascinating to me. I've dreamed about going to Deliverance ever since."

"Those books, what happened to them?" Amma asked.

"Father hid them somewhere. He must have suspected

that I'd found them, or feared that I might, anyway. He wouldn't want word about those books getting out. What if there are other weaklings among the archons?"

Though Gevri's voice dripped with sarcasm, Taemon could still detect the hurt in the way he said "weaklings." It reminded Taemon of what he'd been called when he'd lost his psi: a freakling. Some wounds never fully healed.

"If your father rejected what was in those books, then why would he want someone from Deliverance to train the archons?" Taemon asked. "We don't know how to use psi to harm others."

Gevri shrugged. "There must be something they need to know, some problem they've run into. There's a lot that Father doesn't tell me. Everything I know I learned second- or third-hand, often under the cover of mealtimes."

Again, Taemon and Amma fell quiet. The sun was beginning its descent when Taemon thought of one last question to ask: "How many archons did you say there are?"

Gevri met and held his gaze. "I didn't. But if I had to guess, I'd say there're probably a thousand or so by now. The regular army has at least five times that number training here—separate from the archons, of course."

Again, Amma gasped. Taemon would have gasped as well, but he couldn't seem to breathe at the moment. A thousand! A thousand psi warriors training for battle. And five thousand powerless soldiers, who ate, dreamed, and breathed war.

The entire city of Deliverance had only about ten thousand people. And another five hundred lived in the colony. Neither had an army of any kind, unless you could count the temple guards, who numbered exactly forty after the Fall. Now powerless, every last one.

That thought stuck in Taemon's head for the rest of the day's hike.

When it was time to camp for the night, Amma cleared the ground for the bedrolls and Gevri got out his cooking equipment. Taemon went to get water from the stream.

His shoulder was still numb, but he was used to that. His clumsy legs were more of a challenge right now. He couldn't very well use a walking stick with Gevri around—not if he wanted to avoid difficult questions— but all the hiking was brutal on his legs.

As he squatted near the stream to fill the water flasks,

his left leg gave out on him. His knee was now covered in mud. Across the stream, a group of geese seemed to be cackling over his little mishap.

Out of nowhere, Jix leaped into the cluster of geese and killed one — no, two. The suddenness of the jaguar's presence and the squawking of the geese startled Taemon, and he dropped the flask into the water. He fished it out of the cold stream, and the jaguar glanced at him as she sauntered away. That cat gave him the tremblies.

By the time Taemon returned to the campsite, Gevri and Amma were cleaning a goose. Jix had settled in to a spot on the edge of the site and was gnawing on what Taemon assumed was the other goose. He shuddered.

"Roast goose for dinner tonight," Amma said with a smile.

"I thought we couldn't have fires." Gevri had told them that a fire would attract too much attention this close to the outpost.

Gevri plucked feathers by the handful. "No fire."

"How do you roast a goose without a fire?" Taemon asked.

"I came prepared," Gevri said.

When the goose had been cleaned, Gevri carved off portions of the meat, sprinkled them with some seasoning he'd brought, and wrapped them in a strange kind of paper.

"I don't see how paper can cook meat," Amma said.

Gevri smiled. "Just wait." From his bag he pulled out a box about the size of a book. He pushed a button, and the thing expanded into a cube. He lifted the lid and placed one of the goose packages inside.

Gevri handed the box to Amma. "Here. You do it."

Amma took the box slowly, giving Gevri a puzzled look.

"Close the lid, then push the button."

Amma did as she was told. When the box started to hum, she flinched.

Gevri chuckled. "Don't worry. It's safe."

A few seconds later, the humming stopped.

"Open it," Gevri said, handing her a plate. "Be careful: it's hot."

Amma opened the lid and dumped the goose package onto the plate. It steamed with a heavenly aroma.

Taemon and Amma exchanged an incredulous look as Gevri busied himself with cooking the next goose package. In no time, they were devouring the delicious meal.

Taemon couldn't help but wonder what other surprises they would find in the Republik.

Taemon was licking his fingers, savoring every greasy drop, when Gevri spoke up.

"There are some things I haven't told you yet," he said. "Things that are . . . unpleasant, but that I think you need to know."

"What things?" Taemon asked.

Gevri hesitated. "Things about Nathan."

"Trust me, we know all about Nathan," Amma said. "We learn about him in church, at school, everywhere. Even little kids know about Nathan."

"Yeah, but there's more. When Nathan took his people and left the Republik, he pulled up the mountains to protect it—"

Taemon nodded impatiently. "Cha. We know. Everybody knows."

"And . . . he created a famine in the Republik."

"A famine?" Amma said.

"That's right. Nothing would grow. Plants died, crops failed, people died."

"I don't believe it," Taemon said. "Why would he do that?"

"Nobody knows. My guess is that his purpose was to end the Great War—because that's exactly what it did. For a while, anyway. The war started up again later. But thousands of people died during that famine. People had to flee the region until crops could grow again. And that took nearly a hundred years. The scientists think he used dominion to leach the nutrients out of the soil."

"Maybe it was just a natural thing," Taemon said. Beyond being the founder of Deliverance, Nathan was also Taemon's ancestor, and he felt obligated to stand up for him. "Maybe Nathan had nothing to do with it."

Gevri shook his head. "That's not how the history books tell it. *Our* history books, anyway. When I studied the books that my dad found, they made no mention of the famine. I'm not surprised that you two had never heard of it."

Taemon didn't know what to say. Was Gevri expecting an apology?

Gevri looked away. "The thing is, people here, they hate Nathan, and they hate Nathan's City. If anyone knew you were actually from the other side of the mountain, well, to be honest, they would probably kill you."

FOURTEEN

Plans mean nothing, but planning means everything.

— THE WARRIOR'S SERENITY

"Kill us?" Taemon said. "And you're only telling us this *now*?"

Amma frowned. "What if we'd gone to the outpost without you? You only said they'd imprison us, not kill us!"

Gevri at least had the good grace to look sheepish. "I didn't want to get involved at first. I didn't know if I could trust you."

"So you would have just sent us to our deaths?" Taemon asked. "Isn't that just like a Republikite, to look out for himself and never mind about the other guy."

"Taemon," Amma said, chastising him, "he's helping us now. We shouldn't be too hard on him." She put extra emphasis on that last line, and Taemon knew what she meant: weren't he and Amma doing something similar, keeping Gevri close because they didn't fully trust him? Still, keeping someone close was a far cry from letting someone *die*.

"They might not have killed you," Gevri said, which was a very small comfort. "The archons, on the other hand, definitely won't kill you. They'll respect your skill and want to talk to you—especially my father. Once you get inside their facility, you should be fine."

"And how exactly are we going to get to this facility?" Taemon asked.

"I've been thinking about that," Gevri said. "Do you know someone named Naseph?"

Taemon saw Amma go pale, and by the chill that traveled down his spine, he figured his face was paling as well. Slowly they both nodded.

"A while back, he was talking to my father about sending someone over the mountain—Yance? Lars? Something like that. But no one came, and so my father sent an archon to take someone—your dad, I guess. But maybe you could pretend to be Yance and make up some story about being delayed. From what I can tell, Father hasn't heard from Naseph in a few months, so he'd have no reason not to believe you."

"Yens," Taemon said. "The person your father was waiting for was named Yens."

"Was?"

"Is, I mean," Taemon said, recovering quickly. "His name is Yens. . . . Actually, he's my brother."

Gevri's expression brightened. "Terrific! This will work better than I thought." His brow furrowed. "I guess that's why they took your dad—he must have been the next best thing."

Had they known who they were kidnapping, though, or had Da just been in the wrong place at the wrong time? It was hard to believe that anyone who knew anything about Taemon's da could think that he'd willingly undertake the kind of work Yens had agreed to do.

"What about me?" Amma asked. "Who should I pretend to be?"

Gevri considered this. "You could say you're collateral— Naseph's way of making up for the delay in sending Yens.

As long as you have psi, it shouldn't matter too much who you are."

Amma's eyes met Taemon's. Without her saying anything, Taemon knew what she was asking. As subtly as he could, Taemon shook his head no.

"What if . . . ? What if I don't have psi?" she asked, her voice barely a whisper.

Taemon froze. *Skies, Amma, why did you say that?*

Gevri tilted his head and frowned in confusion. "What do you mean?"

Amma took a deep breath and explained about the powerless colony, about the handful of people in Deliverance who didn't have psi and how they lived separately. Taemon listened tensely, ready to jump in should Amma decide to start giving away *all* their secrets.

"You . . . you really don't have dominion?" Gevri looked devastated.

Amma shook her head.

"You should have told me that sooner. This changes everything."

Taemon and Amma sat in taut silence while they waited for the verdict from Gevri. Would he refuse to help them now that he knew the truth—or part of the truth, anyway? Worse, would he decide to turn them in?

Even Jix seemed uneasy. A low growl rumbled from the jaguar as she sat beside Gevri. Taemon could swear he felt the vibration of it through his shoes, and it set him on edge.

Gevri finally spoke up. "I don't think Amma should go into Kanjai."

"What do you mean?" Taemon said.

"It's too dangerous for her," Gevri said.

"I came all this way," Amma said. "I'm not going to give up now."

"Taemon'll have a better chance of finding his da if he's alone," Gevri said. "If you don't have dominion, they'll never believe you're from Nathan's City. And it's very obvious you're not from the Republik. They'll think you're a spy. You're too young to be a soldier, but not to be a spy."

Amma swallowed. "What do they do to spies?"

Gevri looked serious. "The same thing they do to traitors."

"If she stays behind, she's still in danger," Taemon said. "She could get caught by the patrols."

"I've already thought of that. She and I will head back

over the mountain," Gevri said. "You can catch up with us when you find your da."

"What?" Amma crossed her arms. "That wasn't part of the deal. What if Taemon needs us?"

"The deal's changed," Gevri said. "You two withheld some pretty pertinent information. There's not much we could do except wait. And waiting increases the chances of getting caught." He looked at Taemon. "I'll tell you how to find your father, and I'll make sure you have everything you need to get there. After that, the best course of action is for Amma and me to head back to Deliverance."

Gevri didn't know Amma like Taemon did. She didn't shy away from danger. Together, he and Amma had started a prison riot, confronted Yens and Elder Naseph, faced down two earthquakes, and crossed Mount Deliverance. Never once had she flinched. She wouldn't leave him now.

"I'm afraid I have to insist," said Gevri. "If you want my help, Amma stays with me."

FIFTEEN

The best illusions only seem like illusions.

— THE WARRIOR'S SERENITY

They argued about it for a while longer, but in the end, Gevri's suggestion seemed to make the most sense. Amma couldn't help Taemon from outside the outpost, and Taemon would have an easier time finding his da if he weren't also worried about Amma getting caught and imprisoned—or worse. Taemon and Amma both put up a good fight, but they had nothing better to suggest.

"The archon facility is on the edge of the outpost." Once again, Gevri drew a map in the dirt. "That will work to our advantage, because you'll only have to pass one checkpoint."

Taemon's stomach twisted at the thought of having to pass even one checkpoint. Sure, he'd snuck into Deliverance back when he was a fugitive, but he'd had Amma by his side for that. She made him feel like he could do anything.

He turned his mind to Da. He would do what he had to do to help Da.

"I don't get it," Taemon said. "My story is that I'm Yens from Deliverance, but I can't tell anyone that until I get to the archon facility. What do I tell them *before* I get to the archon facility?"

Gevri grinned. "That is where my brilliant idea comes in."

Taemon approached the checkpoint, where two guards stood watch. He tried to walk with confidence, but the pain in his left leg made it difficult. That, and the fact that he was a Nathanite strolling into a Republik military outpost.

Under his feet, the road was paved with a smooth, hard surface. From what Gevri had said, this hadn't been done with psi. How in the Great Green Earth had they paved these roads so flawlessly by hand? He could hardly fathom it. In the powerless colony, a few of the roads were paved with cobblestone, but most were dirt or gravel.

The guards at the checkpoint stared at him as he drew closer. They looked only mildly curious, but they blocked the entrance defensively with their bodies and held their weapons at the ready.

Taemon took a deep breath. This was where his acting skills would come into play. This was where he would find out if he even *had* any acting skills. He limped forward.

"State your name and business," one guard said.

Trying to match Gevri's gruff style of speech, Taemon gave the Republikite name Gevri had told him. "I'm heading back to my unit. We were on a wilderness survival drill. I, um, got separated from my unit." He tried to look sheepish, as if he were embarrassed by his incompetence.

The two guards stared him down. Taemon put his hands in his pockets to keep them from shaking.

"Keep your hands where I can see them!" shouted one of the guards.

Taemon brought his hands up. "Easy, easy. I look suspicious, I know. It's a spy-training exercise. The captain made us dress like this. You know, so we can go over the mountain."

"Gods, man, you look like a girl with those sleeves. And who wears a scarf like that?"

"Apparently, Nathanites do." Taemon almost smiled at the thought of an entire city full of people wearing Challis's outrageous scarves.

The other guard grunted. "ID card?"

Taemon leveled them with what he hoped was a disapproving look. "Spies don't carry ID cards."

The guards exchanged a glance. "You're supposed to carry your ID card."

"And get caught by a Nathanite carrying a card that says I'm a spy?" Taemon scoffed. "The captain always says that the way you practice is the way you perform." Actually, it was Taemon's music teacher who said that. But it sounded good.

One guard turned to the other. "Did you hear anything about the spy unit doing maneuvers on the mountain?"

"They never tell us anything," his companion muttered.

The guards eyed him warily but drew closer. Slowly, Taemon lowered his hands.

One of the guards started to chuckle. "Whoo! You

smell bad enough to be a godsown stank. That part of your training, too?"

Taemon didn't know what a stank was, but he was no stranger to being teased. "We can't all have cushy guard jobs," he answered before he could stop himself. He tensed. Had he gone too far?

The other guard grunted. "Looks like this little stank's got teeth."

The two guards loomed over Taemon, standing so close to him that he was forced to take an awkward step back.

"What's wrong with your leg?"

"Twisted my ankle up on the mountain," Taemon said with what he hoped passed for exasperation. "That's how I fell behind."

"Looks like you failed that training exercise," one of them said.

"I'm glad you fellas are finding this so amusing," he grumbled. Gevri had furnished that Republikite term— *fellas.* It sounded ridiculous to Taemon, but it seemed to work. "Look, the captain's only going to be madder the longer I'm gone. Can I go now?"

The two guards stepped aside and let him pass.

Taemon walked through the gate on rubbery legs. He'd

passed the first hurdle. Now for the second: find the archon facility without getting caught.

The outpost had more foot traffic than he would have liked. But people here walked with purpose, and most of them seemed to ignore anyone who didn't figure into that purpose. Taemon tried to add a little purpose to his step as well. His purpose was to find Da—and to stay alive while doing it.

Turning a corner, he saw rows upon rows of oddly shaped houses. No, they weren't houses, though they were the right size. They were vehicles of some sort; each had wheels and treads on the bottom. But they looked like nothing Taemon had ever seen. The vehicles seemed designed for one purpose: to carry a huge cylinder. One end was fitted with a monstrous drill-like apparatus, and the other end was capped with a huge metal disk.

Could this be some kind of cannon? He'd heard of guns and cannons from tales of the old world, but they never seemed real to him, more like the stuff of frightening fairy tales. Taemon stopped to get a look. There were dozens of these things—too many to count—lined up on a wide stretch of gravel.

Studying the machines, Taemon felt a familiar gnawing

of curiosity. How did these giant contraptions work? If he used just a squinch of psi, he'd be able to see inside one of them. Perhaps he could learn something that would be valuable to the people back home.

He willed himself into the stillness he needed for psi, blocked out all other worries, and focused on the nearest of these frightening abominations.

He encountered machinery, wires, substances unlike anything he'd seen before. Even though he could see all the parts, he couldn't begin to make sense of them. But these were evil machines — that much he knew.

"You there! What are you doing?" a sharp voice rang out. "Who's your captain?"

Two soldiers had appeared while Taemon had been examining the cannons. He turned to face them, and his left leg nearly gave out on him, his entire side suddenly numb. It took all the mental discipline he had to stay upright.

"I'm with the spy unit," Taemon said. "Just got back from maneuvers."

The soldiers looked him up and down. "Why are you standing here?"

"I thought I saw someone in there," Taemon said,

thinking quickly. "They told us to report anything suspicious." He turned and peered down a row of cannons.

"There!" Taemon shouted. "Someone's hiding in there."

In spite of the added weakness Taemon knew would follow, he reached for psi. He needed something convincing right now, and psi was his only ally. Quickly, he used psi to move the gravel in a pattern that sounded like the crunch of running footsteps.

The two soldiers immediately snapped into action. "Halt!" they shouted, bolting into the rows of cannons.

As fast as he was able, Taemon limped in the opposite direction and ducked into an alley between two concrete buildings. He steadied himself against the wall with his good arm—which wasn't all that good. He had to find somewhere to rest, somewhere safe, so he could get some strength back. He couldn't show up at the archon facility barely able to walk.

He hobbled on.

Someone grabbed his shoulder from behind, then twisted his arm painfully behind his back.

"I saw what you did," a voice whispered in his ear. "You have dominion."

Taemon cried out as his arm was wrenched more

violently. His left leg gave out, and he ended up on his knees. His attacker clubbed him over the head, and everything went dark.

When he came to, his vision was blurry and there was a shrill ringing in his ears. He had no idea where he was. Skies, he hated passing out, and it seemed to be happening a lot lately. He tried to shake the fuzziness from his mind, tried to remember what he was supposed to say and what he wasn't supposed to say. He'd rehearsed it with Amma and Gevri, but that seemed so long ago. He tested his bad arm, flexing his elbow and wiggling his fingers. It felt a little stronger, which made him wonder how long he'd been sleeping.

"Who are you?" A man was addressing him, but he could see only a blur that was probably a face. "How do you have dominion? Explain yourself."

Taemon squinted. Was he inside the archon facility? There was no way to know for sure, and he didn't think it was a good idea to ask. But the man had mentioned dominion, which meant there was a good chance Taemon was exactly where he wanted to be.

"I'm Yens Houser, from Deliverance. Elder Naseph

sent me." His vision was slowly improving, and he could see that the man's expression was full of doubt. Was this Gevri's father, the man responsible for the army of archons? He was dark-complexioned like Gevri and spoke with the same bouncy Republikite accent.

"So, the True Son has finally honored us with his presence," the man said with a mocking tone. "You were supposed to be here months ago. Why has there been no word from Naseph?"

The ringing in Taemon's ears made it hard for him to concentrate.

"Elder Naseph sends his apologies. There were . . . unforeseen delays."

"What could possibly explain a delay of four months? And why didn't Naseph send a message?"

Taemon was prepared for these questions. "He *did* send a message." Taemon raised himself on his elbows and tried to look equal parts confused and concerned. "He sent one of his guards to tell you in person. The high priests insisted on having a say in the decision, then deliberated for weeks before deciding I should come. Are you saying . . . ? Are you saying the guard never made it?"

The man's expression gave nothing away, but Taemon

knew his story's credibility was being weighed. "No, the guard never made it," he said simply. Then, "Ruling committees are a nuisance. I know this only too well. Still, Naseph should have sent a second messenger when he failed to hear back from the first."

Taemon nodded. "I'm sure he would have if he'd suspected anything was amiss. But once the priests voted to let me come, we were occupied with the preparations for my travel."

The man nodded briskly, which Taemon hoped meant he bought the story. "I am General Sarin, as I'm sure you've deduced. As for you . . . Yens. Are you as powerful as Naseph claims?"

Taemon forced himself to hold the general's stare without blinking. It all came down to this.

"More powerful," Taemon said boldly. "Not even Naseph is aware of my full capabilities."

That much was true, at least. But Taemon was hardly in top fighting form—Skies, he could barely manage to keep himself propped on his elbows!

"I see," General Sarin said. "I have to say, I'm not impressed with you Nathanites. When you didn't show, we took matters into our own hands and found a replacement ambassador. But he proved to be very uncooperative. This is not the way we operate in the Republik."

"I'm very sorry about the delay, sir. And about the uncooperative ambassador." Taemon struggled to remain calm, to appear docile. "I promise you won't have any such troubles from me. Sir."

Skies, that ringing! Taemon rubbed his ears, but it didn't help.

"This room is equipped with electronic emissions that block any exercise of dominion," the general said. "Normal people wouldn't even hear that sound, but I can see it bothers you."

So that's what it was. Much better than that Skies-awful serum they used in Deliverance, at least.

The general held up a little box about the size of a piece of bread. "I have a portable dominion-blocking device right here. It's coded to my thumbprint, so I'm the only one who can activate it."

That little thing? He had to be bluffing. How could anything be coded to a thumbprint anyway? The general must think he was stupid.

General Sarin must have detected Taemon's disbelief. He pressed his thumb to the device. Clutching his ears and stifling a scream, Taemon fell back against his pillow. Two discordant tones sounded in his head, competing against each other and making him want to vomit.

The general released the button, and the ringing became bearable again. "You cannot exercise dominion in my presence unless I allow it."

Taemon swallowed the bile that had come to his throat and took a deep breath. "Understood."

"Good," General Sarin said, and got up to leave. "Change into this," he said, nodding at a folded garment. "I'll return in three minutes to introduce you to Captain Dehue. Then we'll see what you can do."

Captain Dehue was tall, with pale skin and red hair pulled tightly into a knot at the back of her head. He'd seen so many different skin and hair tones in the Republik already. People in Deliverance were not nearly so varied. Most had a light-brown complexion, dark hair, and dark eyes — the result of being locked away from the rest of the world.

The general and the captain led Taemon down a gray unadorned hallway, turning twice. Two armed guards walked behind him. The walls were concrete, with metal plating that covered everything from about hip height down. The carpet, which had a shallow but dense weave, stretched over the entire surface of the floor. It was clearly not handwoven, but it wasn't psi-woven, either. Again, Taemon wondered how they managed to produce such things.

At least the ringing was gone. But General Sarin kept his portable device in clear view, thumb at the ready. Taemon had no intention of using psi, of course, but clearly they didn't trust him.

"Here we are." The general stopped and ushered Taemon through a double doorway into a cavernous room about four stories high; it reminded him of the gym in Deliverance where they used to hold the psiball tournaments.

What struck him first was the feel of this strange new psi. The air was thick with malice. He had always associated psi with a certain state of calm. It was the way he'd been taught, the way everyone in Deliverance had been taught, and he had assumed it was the only way psi worked. But there was nothing calm about what was happening in this room.

Dozens of soldiers, perhaps a hundred, were using psi against one another in the most aggressive ways he'd ever seen. They were pushing, pinning, striking, twisting—and those were just the visible signs of fighting. Taemon wondered if some of them were causing internal pain and injury to one another. The noise certainly suggested that: grunts, shouting, whoops, and hollering.

And the body movement! Some of the archons flung their arms as if they were hitting something. There were kicks and chops and shoves that were downright shameful. He wondered how they could use psi in all that chaos—and how they could use it to harm others.

Nathan's teachings held that psi could be used on another person only to assist, defend, or show affection. Even when Yens had wanted to bend the rules a bit, to do something he knew he shouldn't, he'd first had to convince himself that what he wanted to do wasn't morally reprehensible. His ability to outwit his psi was incredibly rare—and incredibly dangerous. Taemon shuddered to think what would have happened if Elder Naseph had managed to send Yens to General Sarin. A whole army of psi warriors, led by Yens.

And the archons were so young! None of them looked to be out of their teens, and a few looked as young as eight.

They had every variety of skin and hair color, but they all, male and female, had the same haircut: shaved fairly close to the scalp, with a point in the middle of their foreheads. The pattern widened in the middle, almost touching the ears, then came to a point again at the base of the neck. It looked as if someone had laid a large leaf on each of their heads and shaved around it.

"Their hair," Taemon said. "There must be some significance to that." The shorn hair was a surprise, given Gevri's long tresses.

The general nodded. "When archon warriors get their first kill, we honor them by shaving their hair. For the second kill, they get to shave the stubble to a point in the front. The third earns them the point at the neck. You can see this is the advanced group. They have all had their first three kills."

"I see," Taemon said, hoping the goose flesh on his arms didn't show.

"I'm not sure I buy into all that True Son business Naseph was always on about," the general said, "but I'm willing to see what you can do. Whether or not you impress me, Yens, you must understand that there is no going back for you. You're on our team now. You answer to me. Not to Naseph. Not to some silly prophecy. Me. Understood?"

"Yes, sir," Taemon said. He'd expected as much. Now that he was in on their secret operation, they wouldn't let him walk away. He and Da would have to escape. He'd have to figure that out later, though. For now, he had to buy some time to discover Da's whereabouts.

"If you manage to win my trust—and I emphasize *if*," the general continued, "you will teach the warriors to work in unison to accomplish tasks that would be too much for one person."

"What kinds of tasks?" Taemon asked, his anxiety growing.

The general considered for a moment. "Taking down a wall, crushing a building, felling trees. The sorts of tasks that will be useful in warfare."

Holy Mother Mountain! Taemon nodded at the general, but his mind was spinning. They'd told him the other trainer from Deliverance had been uncooperative. Now Taemon understood what must have happened. Da would never teach anyone to use psi like this. Never. He'd die first. Deep despair sliced through Taemon. Had they killed Da?

"You'll begin on a trial basis," said the general. "We have some problem archons who are not developing quickly enough. You'll have three days with them. Captain Dehue here will be supervising your daily sessions with them and reporting her findings to me. Each evening, I will visit you in your quarters and will debrief your progress. If you are successful, I will begin to trust you with my more advanced archons."

"And if I'm not successful?" Taemon asked.

"You'll be joining your countryman in the dungeon. Believe me, you do not want to fail."

Taemon tried to look suitably frightened, but inside he was ecstatic. Da was alive! And all Taemon had to do was fail, and the captain would lead him straight to Da.

If there was one thing Taemon was good at, it was failing.

SIXTEEN

Until you have learned an idea seven different ways, you have not understood it.

— THE WARRIOR'S SERENITY

They assigned Taemon a room that felt very much like a prison cell. He had his own bathroom and was relieved to find that plumbing in the Republik wasn't that different from what he had been used to in the powerless colony.

Captain Dehue had assured him that this was a dominion-proof room. He didn't understand what that meant at first, because his ears were not ringing. But after examining his small cell, he realized that everything had been carved out of solid stone. The platform bed, the sink, even the toilet—it was all one huge, thick slab of rock. The bed had a soft layer on top, but even that was somehow attached, as if it had been painted on. Even if he were to use psi, there was nothing to move or manipulate in any way. The rock was too heavy and thick to crack.

Still, he wondered if it was truly dominion proof. Could he take the water from the toilet and use it like a drill to erode the rock? An interesting thought, which he tucked away in case he became desperate enough to try it.

There were no windows in the room, only a door. The door had no hinges, which confused Taemon at first. But he'd seen some pretty intricate psi doors before, and he was confident that with clairvoyance, he'd be able to unlock it. He wouldn't do that just yet. Let them think he was securely locked in his cell. When he was ready to leave, the door wouldn't stop him.

The next morning, he would start working with the archons. He knew he'd have to put on a good show at first to erase any suspicion; Gevri had made it very clear what would happen to him if they thought he was a spy. But how much could he really do with his injury—and with those repulsive archon methods? How was he ever going to convince them he was the True Son?

He did not sleep well.

When the morning finally came, Captain Dehue led Taemon to the same gymnasium-like room he'd seen yesterday, where he met his students. Seven children, all of them younger than himself. All of them had long hair, some in ponytails, some in braids.

"These trainees have struggled from day one," the captain said. "Their test results clearly show that they have dominion, but they fail to exercise it."

Taemon watched the children's faces as Captain Dehue recounted their utter failure. He thought he detected hints of embarrassment, but for the most part they hid their reactions very well.

The captain continued, "I suggest you start with the basics: shoving, crushing, slicing, and the like. And remember, I'll be watching you closely. Any attempts to disobey orders will be met with immediate punishment." She waved her disruption device in his face for emphasis.

The students stood at attention during Captain Dehue's entire speech and didn't relax their posture even after she'd left the room. It made Taemon wonder if they had been raised in this military outpost. Had they ever known their families?

He locked that depressing thought away. He couldn't allow himself to care. Caring meant lowering his guard. And around here, lowering his guard meant certain death.

The students recited their names in the clipped way of disciplined soldiers. All the names were foreign sounding and impossible to remember. It didn't much matter, though; he wouldn't be here that long.

"Saunch," said the last boy, the smallest of the bunch.

"Saunch?" Taemon asked.

"Yes, sir."

"Okay . . . *Saunch*. Why don't you start us off this morning?" Taemon glanced around the room. "We'll begin with something simple: using psi — er, dominion — to knock down boxes."

Starting simple wasn't only for the archons' benefit; Taemon knew he couldn't afford big bursts of psi, but small bursts from time to time should be okay.

"Now, Saunch, see that pile of empty boxes? I want you to use dominion to knock those boxes down. Easy as peas, right?"

"Peas, sir?" Saunch asked. Then, before Taemon could explain, Saunch seemed to catch himself. "I mean, yes, sir!" He jumped to his feet and assumed a purposeful stance, feet set wide. His features puckered into a deadly glare that he aimed at the sinister boxes. It was almost comical. But Taemon knew there wasn't anything funny about the intensity with which the archons used dominion. Even young Saunch was a killer-in-training.

Saunch held both arms close to his chest, then executed an elaborate series of moves, ending with his right arm shoving the air forcefully.

"Eeeee . . . ha!" Saunch yelled as he delivered dominion to the boxes.

None of the boxes moved so much as a squinch. In the uncomfortable silence that followed, Saunch executed a curt little bow, then returned to his seat as quickly as possible. He kept his face as solid as stone—all but a faint tremor in his chin.

"Interesting." Taemon pointed to another student. "You next."

Every one of the students used body movements and shouting along with psi. Taemon couldn't see a pattern in the movements. Each archon seemed to have a different set of motions, but none of them was able to move the boxes.

Taemon glanced up to the viewing balcony, where the captain was watching.

Then he addressed his students: "Could someone please explain to me the purpose of all that yelling and waving your arms about? How does that help you exercise dominion?"

The students shrugged or looked down.

"Saunch?" Taemon asked, singling out the young archon simply because his was the only name Taemon could remember.

"That's what they taught us," said Saunch. "Sir."

Part of Taemon longed to teach these kids the right way to use psi, to bring it out through a calm and settled feeling, not through anger or aggression. Maybe if he taught them the right way to use psi, they would feel connected with the earth, feel a sense of oneness with everything—and everyone—around them, and maybe they would be less likely to use psi for evil.

It was a dangerous idea. Not only was he being watched

carefully, but if he succeeded in teaching these archons how to use psi, there was no guarantee that they'd use their new powers for good.

But what choice did he have? He couldn't very well teach them how to use dominion the archon way. Nor could he sit back and do nothing—not with Captain Dehue staring down at him, watching for any missteps.

He took a deep breath. "Let's try it another way. Clear your mind and listen to my words: The boxes are connected to you. You and the boxes are made of the same dust. You are, in fact, the same organism. You are the brain, and the box is an arm or a leg. You are telling the box what to do. Not pushing. Not hitting. Not forcing. You are simply directing. Influencing. Persuading."

The students' eyes widened. Some of them were shaking. At first he thought they were awed by what he'd just told them. But then he realized they were laughing.

"What's so funny?"

"Persuading?" said one student. "That's not dominion."

"What if the boxes don't want to be persuaded?" another asked. "What if they don't feel like it?"

The class had a good laugh at that. Taemon could practically feel the captain jotting down notes.

"Enough!" Taemon barked. "It's clear that you cannot master dominion using the traditional methods." He glanced up at Captain Dehue to make sure she was listening. "It seems to me that you have two choices: try it my way or be branded a failure."

That chased away their smiles. Taemon pushed aside his guilt and kept his voice stern.

"This time, we'll do the same thing, but no hand motions, no noises. You must be still, silent, serene. Saunch, you'll be first."

Saunch assumed his determined stance and glared at the boxes stacked in front of him.

"Relax," Taemon said. "Be calm. Peaceful. You are simply informing the boxes of their new position. Picture it in your mind, and persuade them to do it."

"I can't, sir," Saunch said. "It doesn't work that way."

"It does. Watch." Taemon stood next to the boy. He took a deep breath, and as he exhaled, he used psi to move the boxes.

A soft chorus of *oohs* came from the students behind him.

"Persuasion," Taemon said. "Harmony. Cooperation." He glanced up at the balcony and added quickly, "You'll be able to accomplish much more with your dominion that way."

They tried again and again, without success. A disturbing new thought occurred to Taemon: maybe it wasn't possible for a Republikite to use Nathan's form of psi. And if the archons couldn't learn to use psi and he couldn't learn to use dominion, how was he ever going to prove himself as the True Son that Naseph had promised the general?

The archons were allowed a break for lunch, and after a quick meal, they had outdoor physical exercise. Taemon would meet with them again in the late afternoon.

Captain Dehue escorted Taemon back to his room for the lunch break. Their footsteps echoed in the long concrete hallway. The captain's silence unnerved Taemon, but he tried to project an aura of calm, as though everything were going according to plan.

A tray of food was waiting in his room. He eyed it warily before finally taking a bite. It was a bit bland— nothing like the flavorful goose that Gevri had prepared for them—but other than that it seemed okay.

His mind went back to the young archons he'd worked

with that morning. Captain Dehue had said they had psionic ability, so they weren't duds. So why couldn't they move anything?

Taemon scolded himself for worrying one second over it. It was Da he should be thinking about.

He finished his food. What it lacked in flavor, it made up for in quantity. His stomach was full, and he stretched out on the bed, intending to use the time before the afternoon session to think through his plan for rescuing Da once he found him.

But almost as soon as Taemon's head touched the mattress, he found himself nodding off. He began dreaming almost immediately, but it was somehow clearer and more vivid than a dream.

In his dream, he was standing amid a crowd that had gathered around the collapsed temple in the city of Deliverance. It was cold, and he buried his chin deeper into his scarf.

Someone stepped onto one of the temple's fallen stones to speak. It was Yens.

Looking even taller and more confident than he had the last time Taemon had seen him, Yens raised his hands to quiet the crowd. Then, still without speaking, he held his right hand over a pile of loose rocks that lay at his feet. Slowly he lifted his hand, and the rocks rearranged themselves into a neat stack.

The crowd murmured excitedly. "Psi! He's using psi."

"It's not psi," Taemon said to the people around him. "It's a trick. There's a thin wire threaded through tiny holes in the rocks. Can't you see?"

But no one seemed to be listening. They acted like he wasn't there.

"As the True Son, I alone have psi," said Yens, his voice smooth and rich. "My power has been weakened, but it has not disappeared. The same is true for you. The power is still within you, but you're crippled with fear and unbelief.

"You have been fooled by my brother. He is a skilled deceiver and a false prophet. Where is he now? Where is he when his people need him most? Is he here, helping us to rebuild? No! Is he at the colony, tending to the wounded? No! He has deserted us in our time of need!"

"I'm here!" Taemon shouted. "I'm right here!"

No one so much as looked at him.

"But *I* am still here!" Yens went on. "I have not forsaken

you. I am the True Son, and I will restore your rightful powers to you and see my brother locked away for his crimes!"

The crowd roared. And Taemon stood at the center of it all, hidden in plain sight.

SEVENTEEN

A weed is a plant that has learned how to thrive in adversity.

— THE WARRIOR'S SERENITY

The click of the door woke Taemon. Captain Dehue had come to escort him back to the gymnasium. Taemon stood up and shook his head, clearing the visions that had seemed so real. Being here, pretending to be Yens—it must have stirred up thoughts of what might have been if Yens had survived.

"Got everything?" the captain asked.

It was an odd comment, as Taemon had nothing to bring with him. The only thing in this room that belonged to him was his scarf.

The scarf. A crazy idea bloomed in his brain. Taemon grabbed his scarf from where it hung on the bedpost and draped it around his neck. "Ready."

In the gymnasium, the seven would-be archons were sitting in a circle on the floor, waiting for him. As they caught sight of his wacky neckwear, they fought to stifle their reaction.

The captain glared icily, which chased away their gawking. "Remember, I'm watching," the captain said to Taemon. She turned and headed for the balcony.

"We're going to try something a little different this afternoon," Taemon said. He took off his scarf and unfurled it for everyone to see. "I'm going to let everyone have a chance to try on this very fashionable scarf."

The archons looked at him suspiciously, perhaps wondering if he was making a joke, but at least he had their attention.

"Let's start here." He handed the scarf to one of the students, who tied it around her neck. "Very nice!" he said, though the girl grimaced. "Now, tell me, what do you think of my scarf?"

"It's ugly," she said bluntly.

Taemon nodded but didn't say anything. He took the

scarf back and moved around the circle, making each student try it on. Most of the archons repeated the first girl's comment—that the scarf was ugly—but a few changed it to "hideous" or "ridiculous." Saunch said it was "soft, but still ugly."

Taemon had come to the last archon, a girl. He held out the scarf to her, but she refused to wear it.

"I don't want that thing around my neck." She turned her head away.

The other archons gasped at her obstinacy, and Taemon had the feeling that Captain Dehue expected him to reprimand the girl. But he plowed ahead. "That's okay. You can wear it around your waist."

The girl frowned and folded her hands across her chest. "Not interested."

Taemon wasn't sure what to do. Clearly this archon was testing him—and he had a feeling he was failing. But *he* was testing *her,* and the test wouldn't work if he couldn't get her to touch the scarf.

"Okay," Taemon said, trying to sound calm but authoritative. "You don't have to wear it. But I need you to hold it and tell me what you think of it."

"I can tell you that without touching it—"

"That's not a request."

He held out the scarf, and after a brief hesitation, she finally took it from him.

"Well?"

She barely glanced at it. "Ugly," she said.

"Anything else?"

"Hideous. Ridiculous. Like everyone said." She thrust the scarf back at him, but Taemon didn't take it.

"Here," she said. "I don't want your aunt's ugly old scarf."

Taemon took the scarf back and hid a smile. His crazy idea had been right. These archons had other forms of psi.

Taemon glanced up at the captain. What was she making of all this?

He cleared his throat. "Today I'm going to show you how to exercise dominion to make your voice sound loud, which is called amplifying." He used a squinch of psi to project the last few words. The technique was complicated but actually required very little psionic energy. It was much too advanced for anyone in this class, so he had little hope of actually teaching them the technique—but that wasn't really the point.

"I'm also going to show you how to keep others from

hearing you when you don't want them to. It's called shielding—and is incredibly useful in warfare," he added, for Captain Dehue's benefit.

"When I amplify like *this*," he said, demonstrating, "everyone in this whole gymnasium can hear me. How are you doing up there, Captain Dehue?"

The children turned their heads to look up at the captain, who nodded curtly.

Taemon switched to shielding: "Can you hear what I'm saying now, Captain?"

Again the children looked up at Captain Dehue, but this time she stared at them blankly.

"Did anyone ever tell you that you smell like monkey feet?" Taemon asked her, still shielding.

The young archons gasped in horror—all except for Saunch, who burst out laughing and then clapped his hands over his mouth. Still, Captain Dehue remained stone-faced.

"Amplifying and shielding can be very useful skills," Taemon said, his voice returning to normal. He rubbed his left arm absently, the familiar prickling numbness intensifying.

Then, shielding his voice again, he said, "But can you see why shielding is especially useful?"

The archons nodded raptly. He knew he couldn't continue to shield his voice from Captain Dehue for much longer without arousing her suspicion. It was now or never.

"Earlier, when I passed around my ugly, putrid scarf, I was conducting an experiment. I wanted to see if any of you could pick up information from an object—information like who made the scarf," he said, looking at the girl who'd told him the scarf had come from his aunt. The girl's eyes widened. "General Sarin knows that you possess dominion, but what he doesn't know is that you have a special kind of dominion—maybe even more than one special kind."

Taemon switched back to amplifying. "Amplifying is something that parents and teachers love to use. It makes them sound important! But it can also be a weapon on the battlefield. If you amplify loudly enough"—he made his voice ear-splittingly loud—"you can stun your enemy!"

The archons all had their hands over their ears. Even Captain Dehue looked pained, he was pleased to note.

"But you can also use amplification to communicate orders across distances—very handy, indeed!" He switched back to shielding: "What did you see when you touched the scarf?" he asked the girl.

The girl glanced up at Captain Dehue. Taemon gave the young archon a quick smile. "It's okay. I'm shielding your voice, too."

"I . . . I saw her. Your aunt," the girl whispered. "I saw her knitting that scarf, and I just knew it was your aunt."

Taemon nodded, then spoke in his normal voice. "Now that I've demonstrated both abilities, I'd like each of you to try. Let's begin with shielding. It's the easier of the two," he said, again for Captain Dehue's benefit.

He arranged the archons into a single row facing Captain Dehue. Taemon stood in front of the archons, his back to the captain. She could no longer see his mouth as he spoke.

"You first," Taemon said in his normal voice. "Try saying something just to me."

The archon looked confused. "I . . . I don't know what to say."

Taemon frowned. "Hmm. We might need to start with the basics. First, try *thinking* a thought that you want to shield. Say it over and over again in your mind till you've got it memorized."

He switched to shielding. "Don't bother with all that. It's for her benefit," he said, rolling his eyes toward the balcony, where Captain Dehue stood watch. "I'm going to try to tell you as much as I can about these other forms of dominion, but she'll start to get suspicious if we're all quiet for too long, so listen carefully."

The archons held on to his every word, and Taemon had no doubt they'd remember every last thing he'd say.

"Two things happened when you held that scarf," he said, looking again at the girl. "The first one is called psychometry, which means finding out about the history of an object just by touching it. The second is retrocognition. It means you can see things that happened in the past."

"I exercised dominion to do that?" the girl said. Then she shot a startled look at Captain Dehue.

"It's okay," Taemon reminded her. "She can't hear you. But yes, you absolutely did use dominion. *Two* types of dominion. You may not have telekinesis—the ability to move objects with your mind, which is the most typical form of dominion—but what you do have is just as powerful. More so, even, because no one else—"

A painful ringing in Taemon's ears cut him off. He cried out and grabbed his head.

"Enough," Captain Dehue called from her lofty position. "This exercise is clearly a failure. Try something else."

"Okay," Taemon agreed, and the ringing stopped. "We'll move on to something else." He switched on shielding one last time: "And we'll find a way to finish this conversation later."

That evening, the general paid a visit to Taemon's room, as promised. General Sarin paced the length of the stone room with his hands clasped behind his back while Taemon sat on the bed, trying to look calm despite his quaking insides.

"I'm disappointed in you," the general began. "I expected more from Naseph's 'True Son.'"

Taemon opened his mouth to explain, but the general cut him off. "Captain Dehue saw no progress today. None. Do you care to comment?"

"I was observing," Taemon said. "It will take time."

"Perhaps you can explain your methods. Stacking boxes? Passing around a silly scarf? Telling them to 'be one with an object'? How is that teaching them about dominion?"

Taemon shrugged. "I taught them about voice amplifying and shielding."

"You *showed* them amplification and shielding." General Sarin's words were clipped and precise. "You did not *teach* them how to do either. Those techniques are too complex for them, and I suspect you know it."

The general leaned in close, his face mere inches from Taemon's. "If I find that you are up to something behind my back, Yens, you will wish you never crossed that mountain."

Taemon swallowed.

"You have two more days to show me some progress," the general said, stepping back.

"I won't let you down," Taemon said. "Sir."

An idea struck Taemon. Tentatively, he asked, "Would it be possible to talk to the trainer before me? The one from Deliverance?"

The general scowled. "He failed. He has nothing to offer."

"Yes, but maybe I can find out what he tried that didn't

work, and then I can do things differently. I only have two more days to get it right. I don't want to waste any more time."

General Sarin paced a bit more, then turned to face Taemon.

"So . . . can I talk to him?" Taemon held his breath.

"No." The general turned and left, the click of the door's lock adding finality to his answer.

The next morning, when Taemon's breakfast tray came, he asked the kitchen boy if he could have some rice.

"Rice? For breakfast?" the boy said.

Taemon shook his head. "No, just a cupful of dry rice to use in my class. That's what my da used to teach me with. I had to learn how to move the rice around without touching it."

The boy frowned. "I'll have to ask the captain."

When Captain Dehue took Taemon to the gymnasium, the rice was waiting for him. He dumped the rice in a pile on the floor and instructed the students to sit in a circle around it. Once again, Taemon positioned himself with his back facing the captain.

"Today we are going to move rice," Taemon said. "This

is how my da taught me. Watch me, now. Look at the rice. Connect with the rice. Tell the rice where to go. Like this."

Taemon used psi to move the little brown grains closest to him. When he finished, he'd spelled out a message: IGNORE WHAT I SAY. WATCH THE RICE.

He made sure to move some of the grains that the captain could see, too, to avoid arousing suspicion.

Conspiratorial grins broke out on his students' faces, their eyes glued to the rice.

"Did you all see what I did just now?" Taemon said.

The students nodded.

"We are going to stare at this rice for the next few moments. You are to meditate as you do so. This will teach you to make a mental connection to the rice."

Using psi, he spelled out another message for the children: IF YOU CAN TALK TO PEOPLE IN THEIR MINDS, IT'S CALLED TELEPATHY. CAN ANY OF YOU DO THIS?

I can.

Taemon turned and smiled at Saunch, whose voice had come to his mind.

Saunch could hardly keep still. *Does that mean I have telepathy? Am I really exercising dominion?*

YES.

Neeza can do it, too. We talk sometimes.

Taemon looked around the circle and saw another child looking at him shyly.

Hello, came another little voice in his head.

Taemon spelled out another rice message. DOES THE CAP-TAIN KNOW?

Both voices in his head were emphatic. *No!*

We'd get in a lot of trouble, Saunch added.

UNDERSTOOD, he spelled out. Then he made his expression stern. "Enough meditating," he barked, loudly enough for the captain to hear. "Now use dominion to move the rice!"

The rice experiment proved incredibly successful. Granted, Taemon hadn't managed to get any of his archons to move even one grain of rice, but he'd determined that Saunch and Neeza had telepathy; Berliott, Cindahad, and Pik had remote viewing; and Wendomer had clairvoyance. Combined with yesterday's revelation about Mirtala, the girl who'd touched the scarf and displayed psychometry and retrocognition, he now knew without a doubt that these archons were a force to be reckoned with.

The only thing he hadn't found was precognition.

He knew what he was expected to do with this information: share it with the general and help him to see how useful these special archons could be to his campaign. But Taemon wasn't Yens, and the last thing he wanted to do was help the general use these seven children as weapons. No, he'd keep quiet for now, pretending to be frustrated and confused by their inability to learn even the simplest psi techniques.

But that, too, was a dangerous game. He knew what would happen to *him* if he failed to teach them how to use dominion—but what would happen to *them*?

EIGHTEEN

Never tell people what to do or how to do it. Give them a goal and let them surprise you.

— THE WARRIOR'S SERENITY

Taemon spent most of his lunch break pacing his small room. Tomorrow was his last day. He'd pretend to try to get the archons to use telekinesis for one more day, then they'd take him to the dungeon, where he would be reunited with Da and break them out of the outpost. But what about the archons? What would happen to them after he left? They would never be able to do what Captain Dehue and General Sarin expected of them. What would they do with the seven "freakling" archons? They were so young.

And he was so stupid! Even after he'd told himself not to care about these children, he'd done it anyway. He knew all their names, and each one had a distinct personality. He hated to think what would happen to them when Captain Dehue and the general determined that they were failures. But he had no choice. He had to find his da. He had to.

In the afternoon session, they played a basic version of psiball, a game that every child in Deliverance had mastered by the time they were this age. Taemon laid a hoop on the floor in the middle of the room. The object was for each player to use psi to roll his or her ball into the hoop. Players could use psi to knock their opponents' balls out of the hoop, too. He knew by now that telekinesis was out of the question for these kids, but they had to do something—and they might as well have a little fun while doing it. Skies knew these children had seen little enough fun in their lives.

Every once in a while, Taemon would stop and say sternly, "Now try it with dominion." And they'd all dutifully act like they were trying for a few minutes. But of course nothing happened, so Taemon would give them permission go back to the powerless way.

"Nice roll, Cindahad!" Taemon said. "Let's see if Wendomer can beat that."

This reminds me of the other Nathanite. Saunch's voice came to his mind. *He played games with us once.*

The other Nathanite! Why hadn't it ever occurred to him to ask the archons about the other trainer—about his da? *Perhaps if I shield my voice, I can ask them about Da,* he thought, moving around the hoop till his back was to the captain.

That was your da? Saunch asked. *The man who was here before?*

Taemon froze. How had Saunch known what he'd been thinking? *Can you . . . ? Can you hear my thoughts, Saunch?*

Yes, sir. I mean, yes, Yens. I didn't know you had telepathy like me and Neeza!

I don't, Taemon replied. *You must be able to read thoughts as well as transmit them,* he said. Taemon had never heard of such an ability. Were there types of psi in the Republik that even Challis didn't know existed?

But Saunch was shaking his head. *No, sir. It's you who's in my head. You and Neeza. And only when you're trying to talk to me.*

Taemon's mind was reeling. Vaguely, he was aware of the

game stopping, and of Captain Dehue yelling something. But he stood frozen in place, grappling with the significance of what he'd just learned. It wasn't until the captain turned up her device and the ear-splitting noise filled Taemon's head that he snapped out of his shock.

"Class dismissed!" Captain Dehue shouted, and the seven archons filed out of the room.

Before dinner, the general made his appearance. "One entire morning staring at rice, followed by an afternoon of ball games. Ridiculous."

"It's how my da taught me," Taemon said. "I thought it might work."

"And did it work?"

"No," Taemon said, knowing full well that the general was aware of this fact. "I'll try harder tomorrow, sir."

"I suggest that you do," the general said. "I need results, Yens! You have one more day and no more. If I don't see something, you'll end up where your countryman did, in the dungeon."

"Understood, sir," Taemon said meekly.

The general studied his face. "You seem remarkably unruffled by the prospect of spending your remaining years behind bars. Perhaps I should have mentioned earlier that we have room for only one prisoner in our dungeon. If you fail me, I'll have to have your countryman killed to make room for you."

Taemon gasped before he could stop himself.

"I see that you're starting to understand. If you go to the dungeon, how long will you have till someone else is sent there?"

That was hardly Taemon's biggest concern. His plan for rescuing Da had depended on their being reunited in the dungeon! He couldn't fail tomorrow, or his da would die. But he knew he'd never be able to teach these children to be what the general wanted. What was he going to do?

"I know you have incredible capacity for dominion," the general said softly. He chuckled in a way that made Taemon cringe. "We had to turn the disrupter device up as high as it would go to suppress your dominion. What I don't understand is why you won't exercise it."

Taemon started to argue, but the general cut him off.

"Oh, you'll use it to do little things, like stack boxes or move grains of rice. But we both know you're capable of so much more. You're the True Son, for the gods' sakes!

You could have torn this place down around our ears! So why haven't you?"

"I'm an emissary of Elder Naseph," Taemon said carefully. "I wouldn't dream of doing anything that might bring dishonor upon his name."

The general grunted. Then he walked to the end of the room and made a show of placing the portable disrupter on the floor by the door. He held his arms out in a gracious gesture. "You are free to use dominion. Impress me."

I could kill you right now, Taemon thought. He studied the general's face, trying to determine if the man had heard him. But the general's expression betrayed nothing.

If ever there had been a man worth killing, it was the general. He was dangerous in a way that Yens never had been — even in a way that Elder Naseph never had been. Because the general wasn't content with just ruling over his own little part of the world. No, the general had much bigger goals. Much more dangerous goals.

If Taemon killed the general, it would put an end to the threat against Deliverance, and to the threat against Gevri. It would also free all those children being trained as weapons. It could put a stop to a war that had been raging for hundreds of years—and prevent one that was on the brink of beginning.

You have my permission to end his life.

Skies! He'd heard those exact words once before, when Yens had tried to kill him. The Heart of the Earth was giving him permission to kill the general, just as she'd given him permission to kill Yens.

But Taemon hadn't been able to kill then. And he knew he couldn't kill now.

"For the gods' sakes, boy! Do something!" the general shouted.

Taemon looked around the room. What could he do? Everything was molded from solid rock. There was nothing to—

Taemon turned back to the general. The man had a gun pointed straight at him. "Do something," the general whispered.

Taemon did the first thing that came to his mind: he used clairvoyance to look inside the gun, perceiving all its inner workings and intricate parts. Then he pictured the gun separating, all the pieces falling harmlessly at his feet. *Be it so!*

As the metal pieces clattered to the floor, a sharp pain

knifed through him. Taemon grunted and leaned forward, clutching his left side. His left leg gave out from under him, and he sprawled on the floor, staring at the disassembled gun.

"Ah," the general said. "Now I see. Your injury is bonded with your dominion. I've read about cases like this, though I've never seen one before."

Taemon didn't want to continue this conversation. Using his good arm and leg, he hefted himself upright and leaned against the bed.

"Yens, you are in a unique position. You have experience that I lack."

Taemon eyed the general with suspicion. "You seem to be doing fine without me."

"We've gone as far as we can developing dominion in these young people. We are now at a standstill. I need you to teach advanced techniques to my archons. And you need me to heal your injury."

"I can't even teach your youngest archons how to manifest their dominion. What makes you think I can teach the others advanced techniques?"

"Perhaps your talents have been wasted on our duds," the general said. Taemon flinched at the familiar slur. Let me help you. My medical officer can repair the nerve damage across the left side of your body."

"It'll get better on its own. It just needs time."

"Has it been getting better?" Taemon's silence was answer enough. "From what I've read, these things only get worse without treatment. We can fix it."

But at what cost? Taemon wondered. "Your offer is tempting," he lied. "But I'm afraid I don't trust you enough to let your people treat me." That, at least, was the truth.

"There will be other benefits as well, just as Naseph and I agreed. You'll lead the archon regiment. You'll have a say in everything we do."

Skies, the man was relentless! If Taemon didn't know better, he'd think the general was desperate for his help. But that would mean his threats about the dungeon—and about killing Da—didn't hold water.

"If I let you help me," Taemon began carefully, "what will you expect of me, exactly?"

The general smiled, though there was no humor in it. "You can't really expect me to give away so much before you've given away anything, now, can you? First you must consent to see our medic. Then, when you're back on your feet"—he nodded at Taemon, still propping himself up against his bed—"we can talk about what comes next."

"I'll . . . I'll think about it," Taemon said at last.

General Sarin's steely gaze gave nothing away, and Taemon did his best to make his expression likewise inscrutable.

"There are things you're withholding from me, Yens. Your injury, for one. And why you're playing games with my young archons. I trust you know better than to try to make a move against me. Such efforts would be futile— and perhaps even deadly."

The general picked up the disrupter and the gun parts, then put the pieces in his pocket. "I'll need your answer in the morning."

And with that, the general walked to the door. He opened it, then paused—clearly aware that Taemon was in no position to make a break for it. "One more thing, Yens. What made you think of taking the gun apart?"

Taemon forced his features to remain blank, but his mind went to Gevri, to the moment when he'd done the exact same thing to one of the soldiers' guns. "It might have had something to do with you pointing it at me."

The general nodded curtly. "A more common reaction than I would have anticipated."

When the general left, Taemon could scarcely breathe.

There was no more time to waste. The general was too suspicious of him. He had to leave. He had to find Da and get out.

Out! Out! Out! his pulse seemed to scream at him.

He started to unlock the door with psi but stopped himself when he realized it wouldn't even be dark yet. He needed darkness on his side. He had little else.

He forced himself to rest on the bed and go over his plans. He would be starting off in a weakened condition, thanks to the general. And he'd have to use more psi than he would like just to *find* Da: telekinesis and clairvoyance to unlock the doors, more clairvoyance to locate the dungeon. All of that would take its toll and bring back his limp. What if he found Da only to realize he could no longer walk? What if Da was in a weakened state and needed him to be strong?

It was impossible. Even if he managed to escape his cell, even if he managed to find Da . . . There was simply

no way that Taemon could pull off something like this—
not now, anyway. Not when he could barely stand.

We're coming, a familiar voice said, speaking directly
into his mind. *Don't do anything till we get there. We're
going to help!*

NINETEEN

When a friend is in trouble, all appointments are canceled.

— THE WARRIOR'S SERENITY

Stay where you are! It's too dangerous!

Taemon tried to send a message back to Saunch, but the connection had been broken. Saunch wasn't listening.

Taemon paced the confines of his room in jerky, agitated steps. What were they thinking, coming to help him? They barely knew him, and they could be risking their fool lives!

Mere minutes later, though, he heard tapping on his door and thought it best to let them in. Using psi to unlock the door left him a bit weaker, but he couldn't very well let them get caught in the hall. Seven pajama-clad young archons spilled into his room and closed the door behind them.

"What do you think you're doing?" Taemon whispered.

"We heard you," Saunch said. "Me and Neeza. We heard you thinking that you had to get out."

Taemon marveled again at their abilities. "You heard right. But you shouldn't be here. If General Sarin or Captain Dehue sees you, you'll—"

"We want to go to Nathan's City," Cindahad broke in. Her large brown eyes stared up at him from her round, pale face. "We don't want to stay here. What will happen if the general doesn't want us anymore?"

Pik spoke up next, his voice a little wobbly as he adjusted his eyeglasses: "Please let us come."

Taemon looked into seven pairs of eyes, all of them pleading. How could he possibly rescue Da and make it back to the city if he had seven kids trailing along after him? And what would await them if they made it? He couldn't imagine convincing the entire powerless populace that these seven gifted archons posed no threat— especially since he wasn't so sure of that himself.

"I can't," Taemon said. "I just can't. You won't be safe in Deliverance, either. Trust me."

The archons said nothing, but Taemon could see how his words unsettled them. Without the hope of Nathan's City to cling to, what was left for these seven outliers?

"You need to find your da, right?" Berliott said, standing tall and rigid in her pajamas like the soldier-in-training that she was. "We can help you. If you let us come, we'll help."

"I can't ask you to risk your . . . your lives to help me," Taemon said. Not when he wasn't willing to risk his own—or his da's—in return.

But Saunch shook his head. "We want to help—and we won't take no for an answer."

Taemon's throat tightened with emotion. He opened his mouth to say something but couldn't find any words.

"Stop gaping like a fish, and let's get started," Pik said. "We already know where your da is. Berliott found him with her remote viewing during dinner."

"You found him?" Taemon was astounded.

Berliott nodded. "I remember what he looks like. That's usually enough for me, as long as it's not too far."

"Impressive," said Taemon.

Berliott led the way. Pik used remote viewing to check for guards or soldiers who would cause a problem, and Saunch used telepathy to relay messages back to Taemon, who was at the rear, struggling to keep up.

Cindahad kept an eye on Captain Dehue with remote viewing. "She's sound asleep," she assured Taemon.

They reached an old storehouse, which Berliott insisted had a dungeon below it. Pik checked for guards on the main floor inside. Wendomer used clairvoyance to describe the locks to Taemon, who used the tiniest taps of psi to unlock them, grimacing a bit when the numbness spread farther down his left leg.

All eight of them slipped inside, and Berliott, Pik, and Saunch went ahead.

Taemon had a chance to rest for a moment while he and the others held back until they got the signal from Saunch.

You okay? He heard Neeza's shy little voice in his head.

He turned to her and nodded, afraid to use any more psi than absolutely necessary. He'd have to be okay. This is what he'd come to the Republik for, and he couldn't let himself collapse now.

All clear, came Saunch's go-ahead. *But the door to the dungeon is locked. We need you and Wendomer to open it.*

Taemon, Wendomer, Neeza, Cindahad, and Mirtala stole quickly through the warehouse and caught up to the others. Saunch pointed to the lock that was holding them up, and Wendomer stepped forward to examine it.

"I've never seen anything like this before," she said, frowning.

"Try to describe it," Taemon said.

"It's not a normal lock with pins and a plug. It isn't a dominion lock, either." Her frown deepened. "There's a box with numbered buttons on it."

"Can you see what's inside the box?" he asked.

"Lots of circuits and wires. But I can't figure out the latch. Yens, how do we —?"

"Hurry," Pik whispered. "Somebody's coming!"

"This isn't what I'm used to. I need a minute."

Taemon stepped forward. "Let me try."

"Are you sure? What about your injury?"

Taemon didn't have time to wonder how they knew about his injury; he was beginning to realize that these kids had talents even *he* wasn't fully aware of. He focused on the lock and sent his mind inside it.

Wendomer had described it well. It was unlike any lock Taemon had encountered, and just as he was starting to fear that it would take him far too long to figure out how to open it, he realized he knew just what to do.

"Mirtala, place your hand on these numbers here." He guided Mirtala's hand to where he needed it to go. "Now tell me what you see."

She scrunched her eyes shut briefly, then popped them open. "I see a code! Four-seven-two-eight!"

Taemon tapped the four buttons. A little green light flashed, and the door clicked open.

"Nice work!" he said, grinning so that he wouldn't grimace. His left foot was almost totally numb.

"Hurry!" Pik urged them again.

From the moment they got through the door, it was obvious that this part of the storehouse was much older. They walked down a damp, dark staircase, the air smelling mustier with each step. Taemon leaned heavily against the wall, praying he wouldn't tumble down the slick stairs.

"We're close," Berliott whispered. "We should stay together now."

At the end of the long stone steps, they came to a hallway paved with the same stone. It was empty, except for the grime and cobwebs that clogged the corners. Taemon felt bad for bringing the children to such a horrid place.

"There's more than one cell," Taemon muttered, his eyes adjusting to the dimness.

"There are eight altogether," Pik said.

So the general had been lying. There was no need to kill Da to make room for Taemon in the dungeon. He wasn't sure why, but the general's lie surprised him.

"Shouldn't there be a guard?" Taemon asked.

"I don't think anyone's strong enough to escape," Wendomer said.

Taemon frowned, but Berliott spoke up before he could ask what Wendomer meant.

"Your da's in the third cell on the right." She pointed down the hall.

Suddenly, Cindahad tugged at Taemon's sleeve. "The captain! She's awake. She knows you're gone!"

Taemon looked toward the cell that Berliott had indicated. He was so close!

"You all need to go—now!" he urged.

"But Yens, what about your leg?" Neeza asked.

"I'll be fine," he said, forcing himself to stand as straight as he could manage. "But if you all get caught, I'll never forgive myself. Now *go!*"

The seven archons hugged him all at once, in one big scrum.

"Just remember," Taemon said, "you're all a lot more powerful than anyone realizes."

Then, one by one, they turned and hurried back up the stairs, communicating the locations of the captain and the guards to one another, acting like a team—or a company of soldiers. Taemon watched them go up the stairs with a lump in his throat. "Skies help them."

As he limped down the dark stone hallway, the only noise he heard was snoring from some of the cells—that and his own uneven footsteps. He glanced at the little barred window of each cell he passed, but it was too dark to see inside. When he got to the third cell on the right, Taemon stepped up to the door and looked through the little barred window.

"Da?" he whispered.

This door had a heavy padlock on it, but it was the old-fashioned kind that Taemon had no trouble opening. He did so quickly, barely noticing the pain that was beginning to spread from his wounded shoulder.

The door swung inward, and in the dim light Taemon saw a figure huddled in the corner, his wrists manacled and chained to the wall.

"Da!" Taemon whispered, rushing forward. He knelt awkwardly, his left leg clumsy beneath him.

"Da, it's me, Taemon. I came for you." He reached forward and gently touched Da's shoulder.

Slowly, the figure raised his head.

Taemon gasped.

The face he saw was worn and had a heavy, dirty beard. He was barely recognizable. But Taemon would know that face anywhere.

Only it wasn't Da.

It was Uncle Fierre.

Taemon's mind spun. Where was Da? Was he in another cell? Why did they need Da *and* Uncle Fierre?

Gradually, though, logic kicked in. They *didn't* need Da and Uncle Fierre. They only needed one Nathanite to train the archons. And that Nathanite had been Uncle Fierre.

Da had never been in the Republik. The "Darling Houser" his mam had spoken of was Uncle Fierre, not Da.

Taemon shook himself. Wherever Da was, he was

beyond helping right now. But he'd found Uncle Fierre! He could save him at least.

"Taemon?" Uncle Fierre coughed, blinking in the dim light. "What are you doing here?"

"I came to get you," Taemon said. He used psi to remove the manacles from Uncle Fierre's wrists and felt his own body wither a bit more. "Come on, Uncle," he murmured through his clenched teeth. "Let's go."

Uncle Fierre was even weaker than Taemon, and the two of them struggled just to get up the stairs. Taemon sent his awareness beyond the door; soldiers were heading straight for them and would be there in less than a minute. He had just enough time to drag himself and Uncle Fierre around the corner to a bathroom.

Taemon collapsed against the wall, his chest heaving with exertion. They'd made it out of the dungeon at least, but now they were trapped in a bathroom.

Uncle Fierre tried to say something, but it came out garbled and he lapsed into a coughing fit. Taemon didn't bother to shush him; the soldiers knew where they were.

The soldiers were outside now, taking their positions.

He could hear their footsteps. He was so tired. So incredibly tired. How would he ever get out of this?

Skies, he was supposed to be the True Son, and he kept getting himself trapped in a corner. Where was the Heart of the Earth when he really needed her?

Are you there? Do you see what's happening? Uncle Fierre's sick and I can barely walk and I've used all the psi I can muster. What do I do? How do I get out of this place?

He thought he felt something. Maybe, just for a fleeting moment. Then it was gone. He couldn't say what he'd felt.

Taemon expected the soldiers to come breaking down the door any second, but they didn't. What were they waiting for? He heard a disturbance in the hallway outside his door. Clattering. Footsteps. Shouting. More footsteps.

Be ready.

The thought came to his mind not as words but as an impression of coiled readiness, of preparing to spring into action. Suddenly the noise in the hallway made sense.

Jix was in the building.

A loud roar that rattled the doors and windows confirmed the jaguar's presence.

Be ready to run.

His mind filled with the impression of running, of legs

eating up the ground beneath them. He could barely walk. How was he supposed to run?

The door burst open, and Taemon shielded Uncle Fierre with his body. But it wasn't the soldiers who stepped through the door. It was Amma, quickly followed by Gevri.

"Let's go," Amma said. "We don't have much time." Her tone changed when she saw Uncle Fierre huddled next to him. "Oh, Skies, you found him."

"It's my uncle Fierre," Taemon said. "Da's not here."

He couldn't bear the sympathy in Amma's eyes. "I thought you went over the mountain," he said, a bit more testily than he'd intended.

"I convinced Gevri to stay," she said, looping Taemon's arm around her neck. "Jix knew you were in trouble. She led us here."

"Can you walk?" Gevri asked Taemon as he moved to help Uncle Fierre up.

"I'm not sure. I can barely move."

Taemon tried to stand with Amma's help, but it was useless. His knees buckled, and he sank to the ground. She had to bear almost his full weight as he did his best to put one foot in front of the other.

Another roar echoed down the hall, followed by yelling.

"Jix can't keep them away forever!" Gevri said. "The back stairwell's our best bet. Follow me." In one swift move, he hoisted Uncle Fierre over his shoulder, ignoring the man's feeble protests. Gevri burst out of the bathroom door and ran down the hallway, Taemon and Amma on his heels.

Soldiers lay scattered along the hallway. Taemon wasn't sure if they were dead or merely unconscious; he had enough to do just trying to stay upright. He expected Jix to join them somewhere along the route, but she was nowhere to be seen.

They reached the outside door, and Gevri stopped. Taemon sagged against the wall, relieving Amma of his weight for a few moments.

Leaning an ear against the door, Gevri listened intently, then whispered, "This is where it gets tough. I'm guessing there are a dozen soldiers posted at every exit. If we can break through that initial clump of shooters, we'll be okay."

"They're going to shoot us?" Amma gasped.

"They're soldiers," he said, as though that explained everything.

"I know, but Skies! Guns!"

"What about Jix?" Taemon asked. "Can't she cut through them for us?"

Gevri shook his head. "I don't know where she is. I can't reach her." He pressed his ear to the door again. "We can't wait any longer. I'll take care of the soldiers. Amma, you look for a gap in the perimeter they've set up. Once we get into the streets, we'll have a lot more opportunities to elude them. Ready?"

"No," Amma said. "But since when does that matter?"

Gevri nodded, then burst through the door. He pressed forward, and before Taemon even knew what was happening, three soldiers had fallen to the ground. Gevri was repeating what he'd done on the mountain, throwing psi around like a whirlwind, disassembling guns, disabling soldiers, sending bullets away from their targets—all with Uncle Fierre draped across his shoulders.

"This way!" Amma yelled, dragging Taemon toward a gap in the soldiers' formation.

Gevri ran backward, disarming soldiers and dismantling guns until, at last, the soldiers were out of sight. Then he turned and ran, quickly outpacing Amma and Taemon despite his burden.

Eventually they reached a hidden glen. "Let's stop here," Gevri panted. "I've used this place before, and I don't think they know about it." Exhausted, they collapsed to the ground. Amma passed around her water flask.

Taemon checked on Uncle Fierre. "Are you okay?"

He nodded, but he looked pale and dazed. Taemon helped him drink some of Amma's water. "Just rest for a while."

"We can't rest for long," Gevri warned. "We need to get to the tunnel as quickly as possible."

Amma cleared her throat. "Gevri, there's something you need to know about Deliverance —"

Taemon spoke quickly to cut her off. "There'll be time to tell him about Deliverance later. Gevri's right: we have to get to the tunnel before someone else gets there first."

"But Taemon —"

"I mean it, Amma," he said sternly. "We can tell him when we get there."

What was Amma thinking, trying to tell Gevri that Deliverance was powerless right now? Sure, he'd helped them escape from the outpost, but couldn't that have been part of his plan, too?

"We'll talk later," Gevri said. "Whatever it is can wait till we're on the other side of the mountain. Till we're free."

Amma shot Taemon a deadly look but kept her lips firmly pursed. He knew he'd pay for this once they got home.

Once again, Gevri shouldered Uncle Fierre and Amma helped Taemon—though her embrace was a bit tighter than necessary. They moved forward more slowly now, the thorny bushes and sharp rocks impeding their progress, but at least this part of the climb wasn't very steep.

"How many people know where the entrance to the tunnel is?" Taemon asked.

"Just my father. I wasn't supposed to know, but I came across the map in one of those books I found."

Amma stopped abruptly. "The books! Skies, how could I have forgotten?"

She looked back toward the outpost.

"You can't be serious," Taemon said. "There's no way we can go back!"

Gevri frowned. "Go back? What for?"

"Those books you mentioned," Amma said. "They belonged to my family. My family's job is to protect them, to keep them from falling into the hands of people like your father. I can't just leave them there!"

"But they're just books," Gevri said. "Surely you wouldn't risk your life for such things?"

Taemon could feel Amma go rigid. "Books have more value and more power than you can possibly know. They're certainly worth my life—and likely all of ours."

Taemon felt caught in the middle. There was only one thing left to do.

"I'll use clairvoyance to see if we're being followed. If we're not, we can talk about going back for the books."

"But that is insanity," Gevri said.

"But Taemon," Amma said, "what about your—?"

"I'll be fine," he said, shooting a glance at Gevri. "Just . . . don't let go."

He took a deep breath and gathered his psi, then sent his awareness down the path they'd just come, all the way back to the outpost.

What he saw—or rather, what he *didn't* see—surprised him. There were no soldiers following them on the path. There were soldiers at the outpost, of course, but none of them seemed to be following them. He pushed his awareness further, trying to find Captain Dehue or General Sarin, but he hadn't gotten much beyond his old cell when a sharp pain tore through his left side.

He cried out and collapsed against Amma, who struggled to hold him upright.

"Are you okay?" she asked. "I told you not to do it. I knew you weren't strong enough!"

Gevri stepped closer. "What is wrong with him? Is he injured? Did my father—?"

"I'm okay," Taemon gasped, gripping Amma's arm tightly and pulling himself straighter. "It's an old injury," he said. "It gets worse when I use dominion."

"There was talk of such injuries in my father's books—I mean, in *your* books," Gevri corrected, glancing at Amma. "Can you make it all the way to Nathan's City?"

Taemon nodded. "I think so. We'll have to go slowly, but as long as I don't have to use dominion, I should be okay."

Amma glanced at the outpost one last time. "I guess that means no books," she said, almost to herself. "What did you see, anyway?"

They turned and started walking toward the entrance

to the tunnel, Gevri still carrying Uncle Fierre and Amma supporting Taemon.

"That's the funny thing," Taemon said. "I didn't see anything. No soldiers, no Captain Dehue. No general," he added, looking at Gevri. "Where would they be?"

Gevri had no answer. They continued on up the hill in silence, taking a much straighter path than when they'd been sneaking up on the outpost. The first light of dawn was just beginning to break the horizon when they reached the entrance to the tunnel.

"It looks clear," Amma said. "Let's hurry."

But something didn't feel right to Taemon. It had nothing to do with psi; it was just an old-fashioned hunch that they shouldn't go into the tunnel. He couldn't know for sure if something was amiss unless he used clairvoyance, though. He knew it would weaken him even further, but if this went wrong, he could end up dead. And weak was better than dead.

"Hold on," Taemon said. He sent his awareness forward into the tunnel. Right away, he sensed something. Several somethings.

The exertion of it made him drop to his knees, even

with Amma supporting him. His vision grew black around the edges, and he fought to stay conscious.

"Taemon!" Amma cried. "What's wrong?"

"We're too late," Taemon gasped. "There are at least fifty archons waiting for us inside the tunnel."

TWENTY

Expect problems and eat them with bread and bacon.

— THE WARRIOR'S SERENITY

"Taemon, you've got to stop using psi," Amma said. "You could kill yourself."

"If we'd gone into the tunnel, we would all have been killed."

"No more psi. None, do you hear me?"

"Yes, sir."

Amma frowned at him. He hadn't meant to make a joke, but it had just popped out that way.

They retreated down the mountain a bit and found a clump of trees to hide in.

Gevri set Uncle Fierre down gently. Unbelievably, the man seemed to be asleep. What had they done to him in there?

"Fifty!" Gevri whistled. "And all of them archons. I could never overpower fifty at one time."

"Is Jix nearby?" Amma asked. "Maybe she could clear the tunnel for us."

Gevri paused a moment, then shook his head. "I still can't feel her. She won't join us if she thinks people are following her."

"We can't wait forever," Taemon said. "The archons will eventually start searching the mountain when we don't show up at the tunnel."

"We have to find another way over the mountain," Gevri said.

"Even if we could find a gap—and I doubt there is one—we're not prepared for mountain climbing. Uncle Fierre's sick and I'm not exactly up to it."

"I have an idea," Amma said, and Taemon could practically see the gears turning in her head. "My brothers used to make kites, huge kites, and fly them by the side of the mountain, where the drafts are strongest. Sometimes they even strapped themselves into the kite and *flew*, which

Mam hated. Anyway," she continued, "if we can build kites, then Gevri can use psi or dominion or whatever to steer us over the mountain."

"It would take far too long to build kites," Gevri said, "even if we knew how. Which we don't."

"Taemon can build anything. All I'd have to do is describe what my brothers did, and he could figure it out." Amma smiled.

"Maybe he used to do stuff like that," Gevri said. "But he doesn't really seem capable of doing much now."

Taemon bristled at the insult, but he was hardly in a position to contradict him.

Amma frowned. "What if Taemon showed you how to do it? You use dominion to construct the kites while Taemon figures out how to make them work. He doesn't need psi to do that much."

Gevri frowned. "I've never done anything like that before. My father trained me for military ops, not for building toys."

"Do you have a better idea?" Amma asked hotly.

"You'll have to draw a picture for me," Taemon said, breaking the awkward silence. "A really good picture."

Amma smiled with relief and scrambled to find a stick

for drawing. "We'll need two kites—big ones, since we'll be doubling up. We can use the tarps we put under our bedrolls for the wings. Here, look at this."

Taemon watched while Amma sketched out her ideas in the dirt, all the while thinking about materials he could use. There were plenty of saplings that were flexible and strong. The scrubby vines that grew along the streambeds could be braided into rope. This might just be possible. But could Gevri assemble the kites exactly as Taemon instructed?

Amma drew the kite in its entirety while Taemon explained how the joints and lashes would hold together. Gevri looked over their shoulders.

"You have to get this all firmly in mind," Taemon said. "Every detail. All at one time."

Gevri studied the drawing again and asked Amma for a few more details.

Taemon glanced over his shoulder and saw Gevri looking back toward the outpost. "Pay attention. Every detail matters."

"I hope Jix comes soon. We can't leave her behind."

"We may not have a choice," Taemon said.

"I can't," Gevri whispered.

Amma paused her sketching. "She'll come."

Gevri turned back to the sketch.

When Gevri had a good grasp of the kite Amma had designed, Taemon pointed to the materials he would need. "You can tag them mentally with dominion right now," Taemon said. "It will make it easier to put everything together later. Connect to them; talk to them. It's like telling them to be ready, to wait for your order."

But Gevri seemed distracted.

Taemon frowned. "You can't think about Jix right now. Don't think about the soldiers, either. You have to clear your mind of everything but the kites."

Gevri scowled. "That may be how dominion works in Nathan's City, but here in the Republik, we tap into our strongest emotions to make our dominion more powerful. Worrying about Jix and the soldiers is *exactly* what I need to be doing."

The image of the archon army training in the gymnasium came to Taemon's mind. What Gevri had just revealed about dominion explained a great deal. "That may make your dominion more powerful, but I bet it also makes it less precise. Am I right?" Taemon asked.

Gevri clenched his jaw but didn't disagree.

"Just try to relax and focus on the objects you'll need," Taemon said, a bit more gently this time.

Amma walked over to Gevri and placed a hand on his arm. "Let's build the kites. Then we'll worry about Jix."

"Yeah, okay." Gevri took a deep breath. "I'm ready." He closed his eyes and took another deep breath. When he opened his eyes, the saplings snapped themselves from their roots and stripped themselves of their branches. Vines braided together to form ropes. Wood shaped and bent itself, and vines lashed it all together. The tarps wrapped themselves around the frames, with vine ropes lacing them in place. Finally, Gevri added the vine ropes for harnesses.

Two large, fully assembled kites lay before them. The process had been noisier and messier than if Taemon had done it, but at least it had been quick.

Amma grinned. "You did it!"

"Did you doubt that I could?" Gevri asked.

"Of course not," Amma said. "You just seemed distracted, is all."

"I need to take a look at these kites before we try to fly

them," Taemon said. He tried to stand but ended up right back on his hind end. As humiliating as it was, he had to crawl over to the nearest kite to look at it.

"Gevri, these joints aren't strong enough. It won't hold when the wind pulls it."

"I did my best," Gevri said.

"You're going to have to do it again. This was a good try for your first time, but you have to do better. Look at the sketches again, and try to get your kites to look exactly the same. Be more precise with your dominion."

Gevri blew out a breath. "Can't we just fix it by hand? Look, I can lash this part and —"

A rustling in the brush stopped him short. They exchanged panicked glances.

"It's them, all right!" an amplified voice shouted.

"Over here!" came the reply.

The soldiers were coming. Their time was up.

"Do it again, Gevri." Taemon kept his voice calm but firm. "Do it right, and do it now."

This time there was no arguing. To his credit, Gevri didn't panic. He closed his eyes and took another breath, and when he opened his eyes, the kites began to disassemble and then reassemble.

The whole thing took less than a minute.

Amma ran to hold on to the kites. Already they were being lifted by the breeze. "Hurry," she said. "Strap yourself in. Gevri, you get Taemon's uncle."

Gevri froze. "I can't go without Jix!"

"We need you, Gevri," Amma said. "Neither Taemon's uncle nor I can fly a kite on our own. And Taemon isn't strong enough to fly both kites by himself."

The tromping sounds from the underbrush were getting closer. "You have to decide. Right now," Taemon said. "You can stay behind and wait for Jix and tell the soldiers that you were our prisoner. Or you can help us and come with us to Deliverance, to Nathan's City."

Taemon saw the anguish on Gevri's face. "I . . . I'm coming."

It took another minute to secure the ropes around their arms and torsos, Gevri and Uncle Fierre in one kite, Amma and Taemon in the other. From what Taemon could see, the kite looked sound, but there was no time for a closer inspection.

"We have to run," Amma said, "and try to get more lift."

It took only a few strides before the wind grabbed them and pulled them upward—more quickly than Taemon would have thought. He felt the vine ropes dig into him as the kite rose.

Just as they became airborne, the soldiers came into view, pointing and shouting. The kite was only a couple of stories off the ground, and already the soldiers looked small.

Then Taemon realized that they *were* small, much younger than the soldiers who had chased them through Kanjai. At least they weren't *his* archons; he doubted the general would send seven duds on such an important mission.

"We made it!" Gevri shouted.

The words were barely out when the air was filled with tiny objects. Rocks! The archons were using dominion to throw rocks at the kites!

Suddenly, Amma and Taemon's kite lurched violently to one side. One of the rocks had sliced through a wing.

"Higher!" Amma shouted. "We have to get higher."

Taemon felt a sting as a rock glanced off the side of his foot. "Gevri!" he yelled over his shoulder. "Use dominion to mend the kites!"

"I've never done something like that before!" Gevri shouted back.

"Try!" Taemon said.

A jolt rocked their kite, and Taemon knew Gevri was having trouble steering and mending the kites at the same time.

Suddenly, Taemon and Amma's kite started wobbling wildly. "Take it easy!" Taemon shouted.

He looked down to see that they were not just wobbling, but wobbling *earthward*. On the ground, the group of archons scrambled to follow their trajectory. More rocks were hitting their targets, and Taemon noticed two new holes in the wings. The kite wouldn't hold up much longer.

"Gevri!" Taemon yelled.

"I'm trying!" Gevri yelled back.

Amma gasped, and Taemon looked to see if a rock had hit her. Her eyes were wide with panic, and her face was red. Very red.

"Amma, what is it?" he asked. When the vine ropes started to tighten around Taemon's chest, he understood: now that they were lower to the ground, the archons could see the ropes well enough to visualize them tightening. The flight of the tarp kites was going to be much shorter than they'd hoped.

A roar broke through the wind in Taemon's ears. He turned to see Jix bounding into the middle of the archons, scattering them.

"Jix!" Gevri cried.

The ropes immediately loosened, and Taemon could breathe again. A gasp from Amma told him she was breathing, too.

The archons had turned their dominion toward the jaguar and were pelting her with rocks, but she stood her ground.

The kites bobbled a little as Gevri watched the battle below.

"Stay focused!" Taemon shouted. Up ahead, a jagged outcropping of rocks loomed.

But Gevri was still looking down. Taemon glanced down, too — just in time to see the jaguar stumble and fall to her side. The archons were on the beast in seconds.

"Jix!" Gevri sobbed. "Jix!"

"She did it for you!" Amma yelled. "So you could get away. But you have to steer the kites!"

At the last second, Gevri pulled the kites up over the rocks. Gevri's sobs had ceased, and all four kite riders were silent as they glided higher, then higher still. Taemon expected to be terrified, hanging from a vine rope this high over the mountain, with its jagged, rocky teeth ready to chew him to bits. But instead, with the soft breezes blowing around him and the sun rising ahead, lighting up the mountainside with pinks and yellows, he felt relaxed and full of hope for the future.

The only sadness was Jix. She'd done a noble thing, giving them a chance to escape. He thought of Moke, who had also given his life so Taemon could succeed. *When someone gives you a chance like that, you shouldn't waste it,* he thought.

As they passed over the peak of the mountain, Taemon finally knew what the word *majesty* meant. The landscape spread out before him was lush with shades of brown and green in some parts, white and snowy and mysterious in others. He caught a glimpse of a jagged stream and recognized it as the one they had followed on the way to the tunnel. The rising sun glinted off its surface.

"Follow the stream," Taemon called to Gevri.

They descended slowly, smoothly. The sign of the Eagle came to Taemon's mind—the sign of achievement, of overcoming obstacles.

"Tell me where you want me to land," Gevri called.

Taemon scanned the tree-dotted land below for a suitable landing spot. When he saw a clearing, he pointed it out to Gevri. "Over there!"

The kite banked and turned toward the clearing. It was small, but it was the best spot around.

Lower and lower they dropped, until Taemon wondered if his feet would skim the treetops. Ahead, there was one last tall tree just before the clearing. If they could clear that, it would be a smooth landing.

Gevri's kite cleared the tree just fine. But as Taemon and Amma's kite approached the tree, a gust of wind blew their kite to one side. The wingtip caught a tree limb, sending the kite into a spin. With much crashing and snapping, they landed in the tree just before the clearing.

When the kite settled, Amma called out, "You okay?"

"I'm a lot better than this kite is," said Taemon, pulling leaves out of his hair.

"Can you climb down?"

Taemon tested his limbs. They seemed a little more functional than before. The flight had given his body time to relax. With careful maneuvering and some help from Amma, he reached the ground with only a few more scratches.

"All right," Amma said, turning around. "Let's see where Gevri and your uncle—"

Taemon turned, too—then froze. Standing before them was a thin, lean man with stringy hair hanging over deep-set eyes.

He pointed an arrow first at Amma, then at Taemon.

"Well, well. If it isn't our old friends from the asylum. Won't Free Will be happy to see you two young'uns?"

TWENTY-ONE

The bitter pain of betrayal takes root as hatred in the soul.

— THE WARRIOR'S SERENITY

Gevri, Uncle Fierre, Amma, and Taemon had their hands tied behind their backs. Uncle Fierre was conscious, but just barely. One of Free Will's men kept having to prop him back up whenever he started to slump.

Gevri had a wild look in his eye, as if he might do something desperate at any second.

Amma must have seen the same thing. "Gevri, don't. Not now." That seemed to be enough to keep him calm for the moment.

Taemon looked at Uncle Fierre and wondered if he even knew where he was. That poor man had been through the flames and back. He hadn't even spoken since they'd left the dungeon.

Taemon couldn't believe their terrible luck—to escape the archons and the Republik only to land right next to Free Will's camp. Seemed like the Heart of the Earth was having a bit of fun with them.

Free Will's men took them through the woods to another clearing. This one held a large grouping of tents, like some sort of makeshift village. They were led to one of the larger tents. Inside, the light was dim. Taemon could smell the sharp, piney odor of the resin that made it waterproof, which reminded him of camping with Da and Yens back when he was little. Back before people kept chasing him over mountains and tying his hands behind his back and pointing arrows at him.

The tent flap opened, and two figures stepped inside. It was too dark to make out their features.

"Free Will wants to see the long-haired one first," said one of the figures. A woman. "Grab him."

Scuffling noises told Taemon that Gevri was being escorted out of the tent.

Taemon waited till all was quiet. "Amma?" he whispered.

"I'm here," she said faintly. "So's Fierre."

"Are you okay?"

"A little banged up from our run-in with the tree, and a little peeved at being kidnapped. But all in all I'd say I'm good."

Leave it to Amma to be so calm under these circumstances!

The two figures came back, and this time the woman told them to take Uncle Fierre.

"Be careful!" Taemon said. "He's hurt!"

"Don't worry none," she said. "We got ourselves a healer."

They left again, and Taemon was just about to suggest to Amma that they try to stand back-to-back and untie each other's hands when the tent flap opened again.

"Let's go," the woman said gruffly. "Free Will wants to see you two."

Taemon and Amma were hustled out of the tent. The sunlight nearly blinded Taemon, but the fresh, cold air felt wonderful. They were led to a larger tent that had a table set up in the center.

Once again, Taemon's eyes had to adjust. He could see the vague shape of a figure seated at the table in front of them, but it was too dim in the tent for him to make out any features.

"It's really you," the figure whispered. A man—and a voice that seemed familiar. "Thank the Skies!"

It sounded like . . . but it couldn't possibly be . . .

"Da?" Taemon whispered.

The man stood and walked around the table. As he stepped closer, Taemon could begin to make out his features. He was older and thinner and had a haunted look in his eyes. But there was no denying it.

It was Da!

"Skies be praised! It really is you!" He pulled Taemon into a hug.

A hug. From Da! His face against Da's shoulder, Taemon took a deep breath and smelled the scent of Da. Felt the pressure of his embrace. This was no illusion.

He remembered all the times he'd tagged along with Da in his workshop or helped him in the garden. All that time spent with Da, and this was the first hug he remembered. Sure, there had been times when Da had ruffled Taemon's hair or patted his back, but all that was done with psi. Psi had robbed him of his father's touch.

Taemon felt the ropes on his hands being cut. As soon as his arms were free, he hugged Da in return. "I thought you were in the Republik. I went there to find you, but it was Uncle Fierre."

Da stepped back and held Taemon's shoulders. "And you brought him back. I can never thank you enough. I heard the rumor that they'd taken Fierre over the mountain. I hoped it wasn't true."

"I heard it was you they'd taken. Mam said they took her darling."

"Fierre was Darling Houser, not me. That's what they used to call him back when he was a psiball player. The best one on the Emerald team. 'Darling' was his nickname; all the girls used to call him that." Da chuckled.

"I . . . I never heard that story."

"It was long before your time. Eons ago, it seems. So much has changed."

Taemon rubbed his hands. "Da, I need to tell you something. A lot of somethings, actually. . . . I'm not really sure where to begin. . . ."

"Perhaps you can begin by introducing me to your friend." Da smiled down at Amma.

"Oh! Right!" Taemon said. How could he have forgotten Amma? "This is Amma Parvel. She's from the colony. She's my friend."

"Pleased to meet you, Mr. Houser," Amma said, extending her hand.

Da hesitated briefly before shaking her hand. He laughed. "That still takes a bit of getting used to for me! But please, call me Wiljamen. It suits me better than Mr. Houser—or Free Will, for that matter!"

Taemon gawped. "*You're* Free Will?"

Da waved dismissively. "Somebody came up with that name for me in the asylum. I was always spouting off about the right to make your own choices. You know me." Da chuckled. "I guess the name stuck."

"But Free Will is a thief and a murderer!" Taemon said, still aghast.

"Rumors, all of them. Ones that *we* started, too. We knew we needed to strike a bit of fear into the hearts of the curious just to be sure we were left alone. And it was imperative that we be left alone. Most of these people were in the asylums for years. They're just learning how to take care of themselves. They're not ready for society—especially a society that's fallen to pieces.

"I'm trying to teach them how to live at peace with the planet, with the Heart of the Earth. The need for peace in your heart doesn't change, psi or no psi. That's what the priests never understood."

Someone spoke from outside the tent. "Ahoy, Free Will!"

"Enter," Taemon's da called.

A man carrying a large tray of food entered the tent. He laid it out on the table before Taemon and Amma. Wild turkey with onions. Sweet tubers. And dandelion greens, which made Amma and Taemon glance at each other and smile.

"What about Gevri? Did you take him food?" Taemon asked.

"Is that his name?" Da asked. "It's more than he told us. But yes, of course, we'll see that he's fed. Whatever possessed you to bring a Republikite across the mountain, though, Taemon?"

It was as good an opening as any. They spent the next two hours talking. Taemon told Da all about his time in the powerless colony and about meeting his aunt Challis, who'd been sent there when she was just a child. Amma told him about the library and her family's charge to protect the books, and explained that the books had been stolen by Elder Naseph and were now in the hands of a Republikite general.

Da listened in awe as Taemon confessed to being the True Son and to speaking with the Heart of the Earth. Before the Fall, Da had been a religion teacher, and Taemon could see how amazed and humbled his da was by this news.

Then, of course, Taemon had to confess to making the decision to take away psi.

"You did the right thing," Da said. "Only the True Son could have done it. Who else knows what you've done?"

"Only Amma and Challis, and now you."

Da nodded. "Perhaps we keep it that way for now. You should think carefully before deciding how and when to tell people that you're the True Son."

"But everyone is so *angry*," Taemon said. "I thought we would all come together, the colonists and the city dwellers alike, and learn to live a simpler, truer kind of life. But people refuse to give up hope that the old ways will return. And now we're defenseless, and a whole army of archons might be headed this way!"

"An army of what?" Da asked.

And so Taemon launched into a recap of the last few weeks, of his and Amma's perilous trip to the Republik and everything that had happened there. He told Da and Amma all about General Sarin, Captain Dehue, and the archon soldiers.

"They know about the tunnel," Taemon said. "At least the general does. What's to stop them from following us here and attacking Deliverance while it's defenseless?"

Da sat back and crossed his arms. It was a thoughtful pose that Taemon knew well.

"Does the general actually know that the city is defenseless? Does he know that you did away with psi?"

Taemon shook his head slowly. "No. I don't think so. There have been no messages from the city since the Fall, and I certainly didn't tell him. Not even Gevri knows the truth."

Amma harrumphed a bit at that, but Da was nodding.

"Then there's no reason to believe that the general would strike anytime soon. He's expecting to meet powerful resistance. My guess is that he'll sit tight and plot his next move carefully. But if what he feels for Gevri is even a fraction of what I feel for you and Yens, he'll come after his son. I can guarantee that."

Taemon frowned. "I think he thinks of Gevri more as his property than as his son. He experimented on him, for Skies' sake!"

"Well," Da said sadly, "he may want him back for that reason, then."

They picked at the rest of the food, and Da filled Taemon in on what he'd missed since he'd been sent to the colony. Not long after Yens had been declared the True Son, Da and Mam had been sent to asylums on suspicion of insubordination. "They separate family members," Da said bitterly. "Makes the patients more pliable."

Apparently Da had been his usual outspoken self, even after his own son had been put forward as the chosen one. Elder Naseph had locked them away to keep them from spreading their "perfidious lies." But Da had organized an escape and had gone looking for Mam. He had nearly been caught a dozen times, but he and his fellow inmates were wily and had gotten away each time. Their antics led to Free Will's reputation as a leader of a marauding group of madmen, which Da used to his advantage, stockpiling gear from terrified citizens and forcing information from others.

"You never found her?" Taemon asked, fearing the moment when he would have to explain to his da what had happened to Mam.

Da stared at the scarred surface of the table. "Oh, I found her all right." He took a shuddering breath. "But her condition was . . . They'd filled her with so many drugs that she didn't recognize me. She didn't even know her own name, for Skies' sake!" He blinked back tears. "I tried to get her out, son. I swear to Holy Mother Earth. I did! But she panicked—and why wouldn't she? I was a stranger as far as she knew. She started causing such a scene. . . ." He trailed off, and Taemon only had to look at his da's face to know that he was leaving out the worst of it. "In the end, I thought it best to leave her behind. I didn't know what effect a sudden withdrawal of the drugs might have on her, if she could survive it. At least there were trained healers in the asylum, which was more than I could say for my ragged band at the time. I posted some of my best men to watch over her. And then I left her."

His voice broke, and he had to look away. Taemon

remembered the asylum where he'd found Mam, hidden away in her room with all those brooms and mops. Whatever healers had once worked at the asylum were long gone by the time Taemon had gotten there.

"I thought you might come looking for me or your mother, so I instructed my men to bring you to me the minute you showed your face," Da said. "But you proved to be just as wily as your old man."

They shared a sad smile, then Taemon asked, "So you know about Mam? That she's in the colony, I mean? And she hasn't woken up?"

Da nodded. "I have a woman posted at the colony who's been keeping me informed of your mam's condition. The good news is that it hasn't worsened."

Da was trying to be reassuring, Taemon knew, but a part of him had hoped to hear that Mam was awake and talking after all this time.

A quiet moment passed as Taemon thought about Mam and prayed she would be all right. "We already lost Yens," Taemon whispered, blinking back tears. "We can't lose Mam, too."

Amma reached out and gave his hand a gentle squeeze.

Da hesitated. "Skies, no one's told you, have they?"

Taemon's blood chilled, expecting the worst. "Told me what?"

"Yens is alive."

Amma gasped.

"What?" A strange mix of emotions coursed through Taemon.

"It's true," Da said. "Yens and Naseph and all the priests survived the earthquake. Apparently the temple had secret underground passages."

"Why didn't they show themselves right away, let everyone know they were okay?" Taemon asked. *Let me know I hadn't inadvertently caused my own brother's death,* he thought.

"They said they were praying for the True Son's psi to come back and didn't want to return to power until their prayers were answered." Da made a scoffing noise. "I think they've been waiting for people to be desperate enough to believe their lies and tricks."

Taemon shook his head slowly and tried to make sense of it. It was good news. Of course it was. But it meant that he would have to resolve things with his brother. It was good to have a chance to do that, he reminded himself. But was it even possible?

When they had talked themselves out, Da led the way across the tent city, which looked surprisingly organized. Taemon noticed that as they walked by, everyone watched them and nodded deferentially to Da.

"How's Uncle Fierre?" Taemon asked.

"He's in rough shape, but I think our healers can fix the worst of it. It may be a few days before he's back on his feet, though. He's resting now. I can take you to see him later."

They wandered over toward the outskirts of the clearing, where they found Gevri crouched over one of his kite's wings, inspecting the joint.

"What are you doing?" Taemon said.

Gevri turned to Taemon with a fiery look in his eye. "What does it look like? As soon as I repair this kite, I'm leaving."

"What?" Taemon said. "You're the one who wanted to get to Deliverance so badly."

Gevri rose and stepped up to Taemon until he was only an inch from his face. "I wanted to get to the place where archons live together in peace. A community of equals where everyone has dominion—or *psi*." Gevri spat the word out as if it were a bug that had crawled into his mouth. "I finally get here, and I find out that no one, with one notable exception, has any power at all." Gevri was shouting now. Curious onlookers began gathering around.

"I spent my whole life hearing about Nathan and his people. How they lied. How they pretended to be allies, then turned on the Republik. How the people in Nathan's City are the same way. Liars. Selfish. Proud. But I never believed it. Nathan must have had his reasons, I figured. There are two sides to every story. And even if Nathan himself had done terrible things, surely his descendants were different. After all, hundreds of years had passed, and dominion would have become a way of life. Surely the people would be happy and free."

"Gevri," Taemon began, "I'm sorry I withheld information from you. I didn't know if I could trust you—"

"Trust me?" Gevri yelled. "I did everything you asked! I led you back to the outpost even though I was risking my life by doing so. I waited around and came to rescue you when you got in over your head. And I let Jix—" Gevri's voice broke, and his eyes filled with tears.

"Gevri," Amma said gently, "I understand why you feel betrayed. But let's go somewhere and talk. Let us explain."

"How can I trust anything you say? Everything you've told me from the moment I met you has been a lie!" Anger contorted Gevri's features. "There is no more psi in Deliverance. You weren't sneaking into the Republik to rescue your father; your father is the leader of a band of outlaws! And you're the mythical True Son that I read about in my father's books." Gevri shook his head, and suddenly his expression shifted from anger to sadness. "But you never said a word. It's just as bad as lying outright."

He took a shuddering breath, then pointed an accusing finger at Taemon. "Only this True Son is not noble and good, like the books said. He is a liar, just like Nathan! My father was right. I can see that now. And when he hears what I have to tell him, this land will be wiped clean of Nathan's cursed people once and for all!"

Gevri spat on the ground by Taemon's feet.

"Gevri, please," Taemon began. He took a step forward, but Gevri quickly held up a hand. Taemon stumbled back. Gevri had pushed him away with psi.

Before anyone could react, Gevri turned back to the

kite and lifted it with psi. In seconds, he had strapped himself in with the ropes.

From the corner of his eye, Taemon saw that a few of Da's archers had nocked arrows in their bows. He didn't need telepathy to know that they would kill Gevri before they let him return to the Republik with everything he knew.

"No!"

Acting almost without thinking, Taemon used his psi to disarm the archers. His left leg gave out from under him, but he managed to stay upright.

Gevri spun at the sound of Taemon's voice. The look on Gevri's face, as he realized what had nearly happened, was one of pure vengeance. He squared his shoulders, then nodded at the archers, who were reaching for more arrows. Instantly, the three men dropped to the ground.

The crowd was stunned into silence.

Taemon stared at the felled archers. *He hasn't killed them,* he thought. *Gevri doesn't kill people. He takes pride in that.*

Taemon looked up in time to see Gevri begin running toward the edge of the clearing. No one made a move to stop him. Quickly, he became airborne. Above their heads, he banked the kite in a wide curve toward the mountain, his long hair rippling in the wind.

At first, it looked like Gevri's hair was getting longer, but then Taemon realized that it was separating from his head, leaving a trail behind him that looked like smoke.

It lasted for a few seconds, and the last sight Taemon had of Gevri was his shorn head. Pointed in front and pointed in back.

Gevri—peace-loving, honest Gevri—had made his first three kills.

Long ago, many years in his past, Taemon had learned not to cry. He had Yens to thank for that. If Yens ever saw him cry, whatever Yens was doing to cause the tears would worsen times ten. No matter how much it hurt or stung, Taemon had learned how to push the pain down where tears couldn't reach. Right now, he had to push deep, this pain joining the one from when Moke had died.

He heard Amma's quiet sobs and envied her. He wanted to console her, but what could he possibly say? Nothing could undo what had just happened.

He felt Da's hand on his good shoulder. "War is coming, son. We'd best prepare."

TWENTY-TWO

Perfect deception manifests itself in two ways: art and war.

— THE WARRIOR'S SERENITY

Da's idea of preparing for war amounted to something like a town meeting. Everyone assembled on a hillside that had a rough-hewn table at the base of it. Da sat at the table along with Taemon, Amma, and the lead archer, Lervie. Everyone else sat on the hillside, looking down at the table. It reminded Taemon of the amphitheater his family used to go to in Deliverance.

Da called the meeting to order and began by repeating what Taemon had told him about his trip to the Republik.

As Taemon listened, he saw Da in a new light. It was strange, how Da was so different, and yet he seemed more himself than ever. The way he was handling this meeting, out in the open with everyone involved, every opinion considered—that was just like Da. Even the outdoor setting seemed to suit him.

"Taemon, do you have anything to add?" Da asked.

Taemon shifted in his seat. The last thing he wanted was to get up and make a big speech. The True Son was meant to usher in a new era of peace and prosperity. But so far all he'd managed to usher in was pain and chaos and, soon, war.

But Taemon was done pretending to be someone other than who he was. He wasn't his brother, Yens. And he wasn't some random Nathanite come to rescue his da. All that True Son business aside, these people were his responsibility, and he could not let them down.

He pushed himself up with his good arm. "It seems to me," he began, "that we have three groups of people in Deliverance right now. There are people in the city who want their psi back. There are people in the colony who want to get on with life without psi. And then there is a third group, made up of people like you, who wish only to follow the Heart of the Earth."

The crowd murmured its assent.

Taemon nodded. "Somehow these three groups have to come together and find common ground. It's the only way we'll have any chance of standing up to this archon army that the Republik will be sending our way."

"Speaking for myself," Lervie said, "I have no bone to pick with the colony. I've been there a couple times on scouting missions, and they seem like decent folk."

Others in the crowd agreed.

"It's the city people we can't abide," said someone from the hillside.

"They locked us away!"

"Treated us like dirt and swept us under the rug."

"Are you asking us to fight beside them? To lay down our lives for theirs?"

"The boy's right," Da said. "Unity is strength. We've got no hope if we don't fight together."

"And what will the city dwellers think of such unity?" someone asked. "Does anyone here truly believe that they'll fight beside the likes of us?"

The man's words were met with cries of agreement.

Da cut through all the restless muttering with his booming voice. "We follow the Heart of the Earth! And this boy—my son," Da said, looking at Taemon, "this boy has heard the voice of the Heart of the Earth. She has spoken to him. If you truly follow the Heart of the Earth, then you will follow this boy."

Wild shouts and cheers greeted Da's rousing speech, and even Taemon found himself filled with a new confidence, a renewed sense of purpose.

As the crowd gradually fell silent, Da looked to Taemon. "Tell us what to do, son."

Taemon looked out upon a sea of trusting, hopeful faces. Once again he felt the weight of his destiny heavy upon his shoulders.

"If we are to have any hope of defeating the archon army," he said, his voice booming through the clearing as his da's had just done—no amplification needed—"then we must unite with our brethren in the colony *and* in the city. For we are all children of the Heart of the Earth, rebels, colonists, and city dwellers alike."

Men and women nodded in acceptance. Taemon knew that many details would need to be worked out later, and many struggles were on the horizon, but for now, the group seemed willing to extend the hand of brotherhood, which was as much as anyone could ask.

"To begin, we must send one delegation to the city and one to the colony," Taemon said. "Amma, would you be willing to lead the group that goes to the colony?"

Amma nodded. She was the logical choice and a natural-born ambassador. She was perfect for the job.

"As for the city . . ." Taemon took a deep breath. "I'll lead that delegation. I'll talk to my brother, Yens, and get him on our side."

"Taemon, no!" Amma cried.

Da frowned. "Are you sure that's wise? Yens is not the boy we once knew. His time with Naseph has changed him," he admitted sadly.

If Da only knew! "I'm the one who broke things with Yens, and I'm the one who should try to repair them. There's no one else, Da," he continued when Da started to interrupt. "You can't risk getting caught by Naseph's men and locked away again. These people need you. And Yens won't be able to resist speaking with me face to face. He won't kill me." *At least not right away,* Taemon thought but didn't add.

Da held Taemon's gaze for a long while, searching for something. At last, he seemed to have found it.

"Go with peace, my son. And may the Heart of the Earth protect you."

Taemon was outfitted with a sturdy pair of crutches for the trip. The healer who'd made them had added extra padding where the crutches rested under his arms.

"Even that will start to chafe a few days in," she warned him. "It's the best I can do for now, I'm afraid."

Taemon tested them out, striding from one end of the clearing to the other. "They're terrific!" he said genuinely. For the first time in weeks, he was able to move with only minor discomfort. The return trip to Deliverance wouldn't be easy by any means, but at least it would be much less painful and grueling than the trip up the mountain had been.

The two delegations traveled together at first, and at night around the campfire Amma and Taemon regaled the rebels with their tales of the Republik.

All too soon, though, their shared journey was near its end. Amma and her group of rebels would go one way, toward the colony, and Taemon and his group of rebels, led by Lervie, would go the other, toward the city.

"I'll see you soon," Amma said, holding his gaze.

"Soon," Taemon agreed, and hoped he was right.

He watched Amma and her delegation go till they disappeared around a bend. Then, with a heavy sigh, he adjusted his crutches and set out toward the city, following Lervie.

He couldn't help but compare this trip to the last time he had gone to the city to confront Yens. So much had changed since then. Some things, however, were the same. Once again he had no idea how he would accomplish such an impossible task.

Taemon tugged at the scarf around his neck and tucked one of the loose ends into his jacket. It was silly, he knew, but wearing the scarf made him feel better. It had gotten him over the mountain; it had helped him understand his young archon friends. Maybe it would help this time, too.

An old saying came to his mind: Just because you smell better than a skunk doesn't mean you smell good. The scarf took away a little of his fear, but that didn't mean he wasn't afraid. He was terrified.

If the people in the city found out that he had psi, and

if they knew that he was the one who'd taken it away from everyone else, he'd have little chance of seeing another sunrise, much less persuading Yens and the other city dwellers to unite with the colonists and the rebels in a war against an army of archons.

There's no way I can do this on my own, Taemon said to the Heart of the Earth. *You're going to have to help.*

There was no answer.

True to their word, Lervie and his men got Taemon through the city gate with little trouble. Lervie pressed a small package into the guard's hands, and they were ushered through without any questions.

Taemon glanced back and caught the guard stuffing the contents of the package into his mouth.

"Honeycomb," Lervie said with a grin. "A sweet tooth is a powerful thing. I could probably tell you the particular vice of each and every guard in this city." He patted his thick coat. "Always good to be prepared."

Taemon shook his head in wonder. "Once we get to the marketplace, our goal is to mingle with people on the streets," he said, "to see if we can pick up any clues about where Yens might be. No arrows."

Lervie nodded.

Taemon, Lervie, and the four other archers melted into the crowd. They looked at the tables of wares spread out for sale and tried to listen in on snatches of conversations. Most people were talking about providing for their families—finding enough food and staying warm over the winter.

Taemon picked up a cloak pieced together from old blankets. The stitches were rough and the patterns mismatched, but it was a sign that people were constructing things by hand, that they were adapting.

The man behind the table spoke up: "That's good-quality wool, right there. It'll keep you plenty warm."

"It does look warm," Taemon said. "But I'm not buying today."

"Ah," the man said. "Here for the gathering, are you?"

"Gathering?" Lervie asked.

The man narrowed his eyes. "You two say you're from the city?"

Lervie blinked rapidly, his mouth hanging slightly open as he tried to come up with some explanation for why they were so clearly out of touch.

Taemon jumped in: "We've been in the colony for the past few weeks, learning how to do things without psi."

"Good idea if you ask me." The man sniffed and made a wry face. "Every day those people gather at the temple ruins and talk about bringing back psi, but nothing ever happens. I'm starting to think it's nothing but talk."

A woman stepped up beside Taemon. "The True Son will be speaking today."

Taemon's heart skipped a beat. Apparently he wouldn't have to go searching for Yens after all. Yens was coming right to him.

"Hmph," said the man. "He speaks too much, if you ask me."

The woman glared at him. "I *didn't* ask you."

"When is the gathering?" Taemon interrupted.

"In about half an hour," the old man said.

Taemon nodded at Lervie, who passed the signal on to the others. Once again, they melded into the crowd and slowly made their way to the temple site.

A sizable crowd had already gathered.

Taemon tucked his chin deeper into his scarf. The air felt colder, even though the sun was out. Bodies jostled him on either side. The crowd's excitement was palpable.

At last, someone stepped onto one of the temple's fallen stones to speak. The crowd instantly hushed.

It was Elder Naseph.

"You know the tragedy that now befalls us. What you do not know is how this hardship has come to pass and how we can overcome it. This is what I have come to tell you.

"We were all—myself included—deceived by a false prophet. I am ashamed to remember when I stood before you all and renounced the real True Son and claimed that his younger brother was the chosen one." Naseph made a sound of disgust.

Yens stepped out onto the stone. He was taller than Taemon remembered, and more confident. He looked every bit the part of the True Son.

Yens raised his hands to quiet the crowd, then held his right hand over a pile of loose rocks that lay at his feet. Slowly he lifted his hand, and the rocks rearranged themselves into a neat stack.

"Psi. He's using psi," the crowd murmured.

Great Earth and Sky! Taemon had seen this. He'd been here. It was exactly like the dream he'd had in the Republik!

"As the True Son, I alone have psi," Yens announced. "My power has been weakened, but it has not disappeared.

The same is true for you. The power is still within you, but you're crippled with fear and unbelief.

"You have been fooled by my brother. He is a skilled deceiver and a false prophet. Where is he now? Where is he when his people need him most? Is he here, helping us to rebuild? No! Is he at the colony, tending to the wounded? No! He has deserted us in our time of need!"

Taemon knew better than to call out now and alert Yens to his presence.

"But *I* am still here!" Yens went on. "I have not forsaken you. I am the True Son, and I will restore your rightful powers to you and see my brother locked away for his crimes!"

Lervie leaned over and whispered in Taemon's ear, "This is gonna be harder than I thought."

TWENTY-THREE

There are two forces at work in this world: good and evil. There is only one place in which a mixture of the two can exist: the human heart.

— THE WARRIOR'S SERENITY

Taemon had no idea how to approach Yens, but in the end it didn't matter. Two burly men grabbed him and manhandled him away from the crowd. Unlike in his dream, clearly Taemon had been all too visible in the crowd.

Lervie tried to follow, but the men wouldn't allow it. Taemon didn't struggle. He wanted Lervie and the others to see that he was going willingly. He was here to talk peace. The last thing he needed was for Lervie and his men to attack Elder Naseph and Yens.

Yens's guards took Taemon to an inn not far from the temple ruins. Each guard had a grip on one of Taemon's arms. He wondered how they felt about using their hands to rough people up. They seemed to take to it surprisingly well.

As they led him to a room at the back of the inn, Taemon caught a glimpse of some of the rooms that Elder Naseph and his priests had set up as their quarters. Fine furniture, innocents acting as servants, plenty of food. The priests had managed to maintain their high standards. Yens, too, no doubt. Some things never change.

The guards led Taemon to a small, empty room at the back. No fine living here. They locked the door, and Taemon wondered how long they'd keep him here, but it was only moments before Yens came bursting into the room, Elder Naseph close behind him.

"What made you show your face today?" Yens asked, his face twisted with paranoia. "You thought you could come back and challenge me again before everyone? Is that it? Well, guess what, little brother? I still have psi! You're no threat to me."

Taemon wasn't sure where to begin. Yens seemed

dangerously unhinged, and if he found out that Taemon really did still have psi . . .

"I thought you were dead," Taemon said at last.

"You *wished* I was dead."

"Never," said Taemon, and he meant it. There had been many times when it had seemed it would be better for everyone if Yens was no longer alive to cause problems, but Taemon had never truly wanted him dead—and that had almost cost Taemon his life.

"I'm not here to challenge you, Yens," Taemon began slowly. "I'm here to ask for your help."

Yens laughed maniacally at that.

"I've been to the Republik," Taemon pressed on. "There are some things you need to know."

"He's lying," Elder Naseph said quickly. "How could he have crossed Mount Deliverance?"

"I know about the tunnel," Taemon said, holding Elder Naseph's gaze. "I met General Sarin."

"You had no authority to do that!" Yens said. "Before the Fall, Elder Naseph and I were working on the terms of an alliance. I hope you didn't do anything to undo all our work."

"There will be no alliance," Taemon said. "Not anymore. Sarin knows that Deliverance is powerless. We have every reason to assume he'll attack."

Elder Naseph's face went pale.

"You told him?" Yens gasped.

Taemon shook his head. "His son, Gevri, told him. We thought Gevri was on our side, but then . . . It's a long story. But it's one you need to hear."

Elder Naseph shook his head slowly. "What have you done?"

"Did you know about the archons?" Taemon asked Yens.

Elder Naseph started to interrupt, but Taemon cut him off. Taemon stood directly in front of Yens, forcing his brother to meet his gaze. "Yens, did Naseph tell you about the archons?"

Yens's eyes darted from Elder Naseph to Taemon and back again. "He . . . I . . . I only knew I was supposed to help operate a psi weapon. That was to be my role as the True Son."

Taemon nodded. He had suspected as much—hoped for it, too. Once again, Yens was merely a pawn in Elder Naseph's dangerous game.

"What's . . . what's an archon?" Yens asked, his voice tinged with fear.

Taemon looked to Elder Naseph to explain, but the old priest kept his mouth resolutely shut.

"They're trained psi wielders. Apparently this ally of Naseph's, General Sarin, has found a way to teach children how to use psi. Only he calls it dominion, and it's different from the psi we know. They tap into their strongest emotions to use dominion: fear, anger, hatred. This makes them less precise than a normal psi wielder but infinitely more dangerous."

"He's lying," Elder Naseph said. "None of this is true. There is no psi in the Republik. Such a thing is not possible!"

Elder Naseph was an accomplished liar, Taemon would give him that. He almost believed that the high priest knew nothing about the general's plans.

Almost.

"What was the psi weapon Yens was supposed to operate?" Taemon asked Naseph, pinning him with his gaze. "What was to be the role of the True Son in your alliance with the general?"

"Tanks," Naseph said smoothly. "We were constructing

psi-powered tanks for the general to use in his war with the Nau. Yens was going to be the one to power them."

Taemon recalled the rows and rows of powerful vehicles he'd seen upon first entering the military outpost. Had those been the psi-powered tanks Naseph spoke of?

But why would the general agree to accept the help of Yens if Sarin already had plenty of archons to power the tanks—and any other psi-controlled weapon Naseph could think of?

Something didn't add up.

"They kidnapped Uncle Fierre," Taemon told Yens.

"What?"

Taemon nodded. "When you didn't show up, they sent men through the tunnel into Deliverance and kidnapped our uncle. I still don't know if it was a targeted kidnapping or if he was just in the wrong place at the wrong time—but perhaps you know, Naseph?"

"I don't know anything about a kidnapping. I've been stationed in this inn since the Fall, working with the True Son to help restore his psi. We have been incredibly successful. He is nearly—"

"Enough!" Taemon shouted, his body going rigid with

rage. "Enough lies! I know about the deal you struck with the general, Naseph. Yens was to train his army of archons to be their deadliest." His mouth twisted with disgust. "I don't know what you were getting out of the deal—protection, maybe, when the war spread beyond the borders of the Republik?—but you and I both know that the general's archons are a formidable force. One that we can't simply ignore."

Finally, the full weight of the situation seemed to be dawning on the high priest. He shifted uncomfortably. "Perhaps when they see what Yens can do—" he began feebly.

"Yens has no more psi than you do."

"That's not true!" Yens protested. "I—"

"Tricks. Sleights of hand," Taemon interrupted dismissively. "Did you really think such things could fool *me*, Yens?" Taemon had mastered such tricks when he'd first lost his psi—and Yens well knew it.

"So what is it that you want, exactly?" Naseph asked carefully.

"I want to create an alliance of our own—among your followers here in the city, the people in the colony, and Free Will's men."

"Free Will's men?" Yens asked. "Those miscreants? Why would we possibly want to ally with them?"

"Those . . . miscreants, as you put it, are being led by our father."

Yens looked shocked. Elder Naseph, however, barely reacted.

"You knew?" Yens asked Naseph. "And you never said anything? We've got a reward out for Free Will's head!"

"I wanted to spare you that pain," Elder Naseph said. "Those people are escaped asylum inmates. They pose a danger to themselves and to others—Free Will especially."

"But that's my *da*!" Yens said.

"It's okay," Taemon said. "Da's safe for now. I've just come from him. But if we're going to have any hope of fending off the archons, we'll need to work together. All of us."

"Even if we do join forces, how can we possibly hold back the general's army?" Naseph asked. "We're like ripe berries for the picking."

Taemon braced himself for what he had to say next.

"I . . . I still have psi."

•   •   •

They'd asked him to prove it, and Taemon had done just enough to put their doubts to rest while minimizing the physical strain on himself.

Yens narrowed his eyes. "Isn't that exactly like you? To take everyone's powers away except your own. You've always had a complex about being a weak freak. You just had to tear everyone else down to make yourself feel strong."

"I never wanted this!" Taemon protested, though he knew it was futile. "I wanted to usher in a new era where we would all work together and live as the Heart of the Earth intended."

"You presume to know what the Heart of the Earth intends, boy?" Elder Naseph asked, pulling himself up and looking every bit like the fearsome high priest he was. "The Heart of the Earth chose Nathan and his people to have psi! She wanted us to embrace our gifts, not toss them aside like rubbish! How *dare* you stand before me and tell me—"

"Now is not the time to debate religion, Naseph," Taemon snapped. If only his da could see him now, standing up to the high priest! "We cannot undo what has already been done. But what we can do is try to minimize the future damage."

"So what do you propose?" Naseph asked, his jaw tight.

Taemon explained his plan for fighting off the archons. All the while, the muscles in Yens's jaw were working, his face reddening.

"This is exactly what I was afraid of!" Yens exploded when Taemon was done. "You've set everything up so you can be the big hero. Skies, Taemon, how many people have to suffer so you can feel important?"

Taemon sighed with exasperation. "I'm the only one who has psi. What else do you suggest?"

Yens's expression turned calculating. "I'll go along with your plan on one condition: whatever psi you wield during the battle, you make it look like I'm the one with psi. When this is all over and done with, I want there to be no doubt in anyone's mind that *I* am the True Son."

"Why does the True Son matter now?" Taemon asked. "If this doesn't work, we could all be dead!"

"But if it *does* work," Yens said, "the people will want someone to thank. And I want that someone to be me."

"Fine," Taemon said. "I'll make it look like you're the one with the power."

Why not let Yens take the credit? It wasn't like Taemon himself wanted the attention. And while Yens might be held up as a hero after the battle was over—assuming they were successful, of course—he still wouldn't have psi. He'd be the True Son in name only.

What harm could there be in that?

TWENTY-FOUR

To be indecisive is to divide your energy and weaken your desire.

— THE WARRIOR'S SERENITY

Over the next few days, Taemon and Yens worked together surprisingly well. The promise of future glory clearly was a strong motivator for Yens; he listened to Taemon's ideas and followed Taemon's instructions, even when Elder Naseph grumbled and resisted.

For the standoff, Taemon chose the place in the hills where the archon army was most likely to emerge.

"This is where the True Son will take his stand to defend his people," Yens said reverently, likely already picturing his supposed acts of heroism.

Amma clearly had done her job as a delegate. Hannova sent a sizable group of men and women from the colony, along with the powerless logging equipment. Amma came with them and began giving the colonists assignments to work alongside the city dwellers.

Yens and Elder Naseph recruited an impressively large group of city dwellers. They worked together to dig a huge pit, which was quite an ordeal because the city dwellers had never shoveled without psi before. Amma paired each colonist with a city dweller so that the colonists could demonstrate how to force the shovel into the soil and then use the handle as a lever to loosen the dirt. Taemon was amazed at how long it took to move that much dirt without psi. But they got it done.

Another group worked on stacking boulders on the slopes of the hills. Again, the colonists had to divide up and show the city dwellers how to use simple machines like inclined planes and levers to position the boulders just so.

Yens worked with some of Free Will's men to build a tower where the True Son would stand. Taemon had sent Lervie to tell Da not to show his face just yet; he didn't trust Naseph not to take advantage of this opportunity to get rid of Da in a supposed "accident." Instead, Taemon suggested that Da go to the colony and stay with Mam. Perhaps hearing his voice would be enough to wake her.

The tower was a risky tactic, because if the archons could see Yens, they could use psi to attack him. On the other hand, Taemon's plan relied on the archons assuming that Yens was using psi, and that meant Yens had to be out in the open.

Fortunately, using psi over long distances was difficult even under the best circumstances. The archons, fueling their dominion with anger and hatred, would be even less likely to do much damage from afar. Taemon would just have to repel the archons before they got too close.

"Are you sure about this?" Amma asked him as they inspected the battlefield late one afternoon. The ditches had all been dug, the tower had been erected, and the old quadriders had been buried. All that was left now was for the enemy to show up.

Taemon shrugged. "It's the best we could do under the circumstances."

Amma was quiet for a moment. When she spoke again, her voice was teary. "You're putting yourself in a great deal of danger. You've heard what the healers said about using so much psi—"

"I don't have a choice," he said. "I can't just sit back and watch my people get slaughtered. It's my fault they're all powerless. I have to do whatever I can to protect them. Even if . . . even if it means giving up my life."

Amma took his right hand in hers and gave it a squeeze. They walked hand in hand through the growing darkness.

Two days later, the word came from the scouts Lervie had posted: the archons had been sighted, and they were on their way down the mountain.

From his vantage point on a small platform hidden in a tree near the tower, Taemon took stock. The boulders were in place. The ditches had been camouflaged well. The quadriders were covered up. And Yens was climbing the ladder to his tower. Everything looked ready.

But would it be enough?

"Are you absolutely sure about all this arm-waving stuff?" Yens asked Taemon from the tower. "It feels ridiculous."

"That's how they do things," Taemon assured him. "They'll think you're the one using dominion if they see you doing what they do."

"If this is some trick to make me look like a fool . . ." Yens began.

"When this is all over, you won't look foolish," Taemon said. "You'll look like a hero."

"You'd better be right," Yens said. "All right, everyone!" he called out, with Taemon amplifying his voice. "Today Deliverance must earn its name once again. The Heart of the Earth will deliver her people from the hands of her enemies!"

A cheer rose from the people below, concealed throughout the battlefield. People from the city, from the colony, and from Da's band of rebels had all taken their positions. Everyone had a role to play. They'd worked together to prepare the battlefield, and now they were ready to fight— and die if necessary. But Taemon prayed it wouldn't come to that.

As the cheering died down, Taemon heard the sound of someone climbing the ladder to the platform. Amma appeared and scrambled up beside him.

"I came to keep an eye on the True Son," she said. "The real one, I mean."

"You don't have to do that," Taemon said. "I'll be fine." He'd been resting up for this. His limp had been much better recently, and his shoulder hadn't felt this good since the arrow had done its damage.

Amma leveled him with a look. "Do you really expect me to just hide myself in the brush while you're up here risking your life? The least I can do is be another pair of eyes for you."

She made a good point. And while Taemon wouldn't ever admit it, he felt better with Amma at his side.

"Look!" Amma said, pointing. Taemon squinted. The first archon was coming down the trail.

"Get ready!" he called up to Yens.

The archon drew closer. He appeared to be alone, though maybe he was just a scout sent to make sure the coast was clear.

Amma gasped. Taemon strained to get a better look at the archon. Suddenly, he recognized him.

It was Gevri.

Taemon watched as Gevri spotted Yens on the tower. He turned and shouted something. Even though he was using amplification, he was still too far away for Taemon to make out his words.

But soon the message became apparent. Dozens of archons appeared behind Gevri. Taemon tried to count them as they streamed down the hill. There had to be more than a hundred—not the full thousand that Gevri had described, but plenty daunting even so.

They must have thought Deliverance would be an easy target. Taemon hoped that the people of Deliverance would prove them wrong.

When the archons reached the spot that Taemon and Yens had agreed upon earlier, Yens began waving his arms as if directing traffic.

Now for some psi.

Taemon pictured the boulders they'd stacked on the hillside. Then he imagined them cascading toward the archons. *Be it so!*

Taemon doubled over as a burning pain passed through his left side. But he had expected that. And there was more to come, so he steeled himself and locked away the pain.

Amma held his arm. "The boulders were perfect! The archons are headed right toward the quadriders."

She was right. The boulders had forced the archons to veer off to the left—exactly where they wanted them.

Taemon glanced at Yens, who was now stretching his arms forward and shaking his hands, which was the signal for the next trick.

Taemon pictured in his mind the old quadriders that had been buried under the ground where the archons now stood. Using psi, he made the quadriders shake and bounce in place. The earth shifted and quivered under the archons' feet—a fairly impressive replica of an earthquake.

The archons stopped in bewilderment.

Yens waved his hand madly, and Taemon obliged by sending even more psi at the quadriders, which now banged and knocked against one another under the ground. The muffled sound was truly terrifying—as if the Heart of the Earth herself were crying out in rage.

Taemon's vision blurred, and his legs buckled. Amma helped him sit down.

"What's happening?" Taemon said. "I can't see."

Amma's answer was calm and steady. "The archons are scattering, looking for cover. They're confused."

Of course they were confused. They had been expecting to easily overtake the powerless people of Deliverance. Now they were seeing some frightening displays of power.

There's more to come, Taemon thought. *I know what you fear most.*

"Keep going!" a familiar voice shouted. Gevri. "Don't stop!"

Taemon heard the roar of the approaching archons. Then there was a splintering sound nearby. "Is that the tower?"

"Cha, they've stripped away the false front," Amma said.

It had been Amma's suggestion to build a false front on the tower to hide its true supporting framework. This would buy them a bit more time should the archons advance close enough to begin dismantling the tower.

They'd come closer much more quickly than Taemon had anticipated, but Amma claimed it was only a handful of archons who'd advanced this far.

"Gevri's trying to coax the others away from the trees where they've hidden themselves," Amma said.

"Watch Yens," Taemon said. "Tell me when he gives the final signal." They had one more big trick up their sleeve.

If this didn't turn the archons back, the people hidden in the brush would be forced into hand-to-hand combat. Taemon didn't want to think of what would happen then.

"There!" Amma cried. "He's given the signal. Be careful, Taemon."

Time for the grand finale. He prayed it would actually work.

Using clairvoyance, he reached out with his awareness to locate the archons, relieved to find that he could manage it even though he couldn't see. He sent his psi farther and connected to the plants near them. First, the grass. Taemon pictured it fading, withering, and crumbling into dust. *Be it so!*

"Oh!" Amma gasped.

Taemon was on the edge of consciousness.

"The famine!" someone cried. "The Nathanites mean to cause another famine!"

"No!" It was Gevri now. "We are not turning back! Kanjai is safe! Let them poison their own fields for all we care! We will fight!"

"But you said they had no dominion! You said they were powerless!" another voice shouted.

An angry murmur came from below, and Taemon could easily envision the breakdown of the careful military formations.

"What does that matter?" Gevri cried back. "They lied to us, just as a Nathanite would. They have dominion, yes, but so do we! This fight is not over!"

A creaky groan came from the tower, and Taemon knew he would have to do more. He reached down, further down, and summoned all the strength he had.

A feeling stirred in his heart, a sense of rightness. He was doing what the Heart of the Earth wanted. He would give his life for his people, and it would be worth it. This was what the True Son was meant to do all along.

He pictured the evergreen trees that lined the valley. He saw them turning brown, withering, and dying. *Be it so!*

When he heard the gasps, he knew it had worked. He opened his eyes and was surprised to find that he could see clearly. In fact, he felt stronger than he had in a long time. The pain in his left side was completely gone, as if it had never been there.

He stood up, and Amma, looking rather astonished, rose with him.

"You were wrong, Gevri!" Taemon heard from below. "The people of Nathan's City are not weak. They are strong—stronger than we are!"

One by one the archons turned and ran back up the trail, the grass and trees dying as they passed them.

Deserted by his archon army, Gevri turned to face the tower. "Hear me! This nation of deceivers will not stand! The Republik will take its rightful place as rulers. And I will return to see every last Nathanite dead!"

With one last roar of frustration, he turned and headed for the tunnel.

TWENTY-FIVE

An end is only a beginning in disguise.

— THE WARRIOR'S SERENITY

Yens held both arms skyward. "The True Son has led his people to victory!"

The people came pouring out from behind rocks, brush, and trees, cheering and roaring and whooping. "Yens! Yens! Yens!"

Taemon was reminded of the psiball tournaments he used to attend, when the crowds would also chant his brother's name. Only this time, he felt not even the slightest squinch of jealousy.

Let Yens have his spotlight. Taemon had ensured the safety of his people. That was all he needed to be content.

The True Son has led his people to victory.

Though the Heart of the Earth repeated Yens's words, Taemon knew they were meant for him.

Thank you for healing me, Taemon responded.

The injury was a manifestation of your divided heart. Once you held to one desire above all others, your psi and your body became reconciled.

Is it finished? Have I done what you wanted? he asked her. But of course there was no answer.

"It worked," Amma whispered, looking out over the little valley, shriveled and brown, a sacrifice from the Heart of the Earth for her people. "I honestly didn't know if it would, but it did."

She turned to him and touched his shoulder. "And look at you, standing there without even a slouch. I thought I'd have to peel you off the floor by now."

Taemon could see the true concern behind her light words. He knew she'd feared it would be much worse than that.

He massaged his shoulder, then worked the fingers of his left hand. "It's healed. Completely."

"That's . . . convenient," Amma said.

He nodded. If he hadn't gotten stronger right when he had . . . It didn't bear thinking about. He didn't know if the Heart of the Earth's explanation would make sense to Amma. He had a feeling those words were meant for him alone.

She sighed. "Poor Gevri. He's so angry. I wish there were a way to talk with him, to explain why we did the things we did. Even if he never forgave us, he might at least come to understand us."

Taemon looked at Mount Deliverance, at the snowy ridges and evergreens dotting its side. He was glad he'd had to sacrifice only a few of those magnificent trees.

Suddenly, another sight filled his vision: the Republikite tanks, those monstrosities with mounted cannons, crashing through these same trees.

As quickly as it had come, though, the vision left.

Taemon shook his head. "I have a feeling the time for talking has passed," he said grimly.

He'd tell her—and the others—what he'd seen later. For now, they had a victory to celebrate.

ACKNOWLEDGMENTS

A zillion thank-yous to Kaylan Adair, Maryellen Hanley, and everyone at Candlewick Press for their wonderful work. I want to thank Molly Jaffa and the fantastic Folio team for all their support. I appreciate the help and encouragement of my fabulous family and friends.

I am lucky to live in a place where local writers are supported in many ways. Thank you to everyone at Richmond Children's Writers, James River Writers, SCBWI Mid-Atlantic region, bbgb tales for kids, Fountain Bookstore, many librarians and teachers, and all the amazing young readers out there!